/250

POET
······ AND ······
DANCER

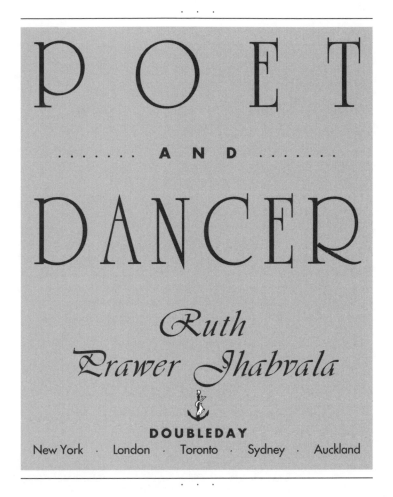

POET

AND

DANCER

Ruth Prawer Jhabvala

DOUBLEDAY

New York · London · Toronto · Sydney · Auckland

PUBLISHED BY DOUBLEDAY
a division of
Bantam Doubleday Dell Publishing Group, Inc.
666 Fifth Avenue, New York, New York 10103

DOUBLEDAY and the portrayal of an anchor
with a dolphin are trademarks of Doubleday,
a division of Bantam Doubleday Dell Publishing Group, Inc.

Book design by Guenet Abraham

Library of Congress Cataloging-in-Publication Data

Jhabvala, Ruth Prawer, 1927–
Poet and dancer / by Ruth Prawer Jhabvala. — 1st ed.
        p.   cm.
        I. Title.
    PR9499.3.J5P63   1993
    823—dc20   92-22945
                                             CIP

ISBN 0-385-46869-5
Printed in the United States of America

March 1993

1   3   5   7   9   10   8   6   4   2

First Edition

POET

AND

DANCER

Foreword

SOME YEARS AGO I became involved in the psycho-evolutionary work of Dr. Hugo Manarr. He was by then no longer at the height of his career—that had been twenty to thirty years earlier—but he still had a group of followers who practiced his methods of self-perfection. It was a time in my life when I was looking for someone's guidance, and he was only one of several teachers whom I tried out and, I must admit, dropped in disappointment. The disappointment was probably with myself and not with him or the others, but that is a story I have told elsewhere, and more than once.

The events narrated here are connected not with myself but with Dr. Manarr and some members of his family. I never met the principal protagonists—that is, Dr. Manarr's own daughter and his sister's daughter. I did meet his sister,

Helena Manarr (she never used her married name of Koenig), and got to know her better than I did Dr. Manarr himself. He was always charming but not really approachable except by his team of blond and buxom girlfriends known as the Valkyries. I never heard him mention his daughter, and I suspect no one else did, perhaps not even the Valkyrie whom he eventually married.

I first saw Helena Manarr in the Fifth Avenue apartment that was her brother's home and place of work. I believe she was living with him at the time, in between one of her many moves. Although she never stayed anywhere for long, she always rented in the same neighborhood of West Side apartment complexes built some twenty-five years earlier. This was where her daughter had lived with Dr. Manarr's daughter. When I met her, Helena had long since sold her family house on the East Side with all its furniture, as well as her business. She was no longer in touch with her Indian business partner—nor, as far as I could see, with anyone she had ever known. Except for her visits to her brother, she lived in complete solitude.

She was an odd contrast to the students and followers who came to Dr. Manarr's apartment. They were all set on a course of self-perfection, and the work they did on themselves made their eyes and their complexions seem very bright—an impression enhanced by the youthful clothes worn even by those of them who were no longer youthful. Helena's dresses were black but appeared to be grayish, with dust, and sometimes had crumbs scattered over them, and there were always one or two strands of her long white hair clinging to the fabric. She carried a large handbag out of which she pulled things and dropped them, so that she was often grabbling around on the floor. If anyone helped her, she quickly snatched whatever they had found out of their hands to stuff it back into her bag. She never seemed to communicate with anyone, not even by looking at them. There was something shifty about her—literally, insofar as her eyes shifted away from meeting anyone else's, as though she were afraid or ashamed. She gave the impression of a somewhat mad or at least eccentric old woman—she was well into her seventies—and also that she was unwilling for anyone to speak to her. Most people, including myself, did not often try.

But one day, when I left Dr. Manarr's study after working with him, she came up to me and said, quite eagerly, "Hugo has told me you're a writer." She seemed to have been waiting for me, and we went down in the elevator together; she had put on a hat as large and black as her handbag. She said, "My daughter was a writer." Her face under the hat lit up. "She was a poet." When she spoke of her daughter, she took on a feverish vitality. She also exerted such a force of will that I felt compelled to stay and listen to her, even though I had an appointment to keep in the opposite direction. She said, "Would you like to see her poems?" She meant there and then and stood still on the sidewalk, just by the canopy of an apartment building with splendid doormen eyeing us. She thrust her hand into her bag, and while I expected the usual shower of keys, glasses, and cash memos, she came up at once with a sheaf of copybook pages fastened together. She held them up for me to see, smiling coyly as though handing out a treat, only to withdraw them and stuff them back. She didn't even have to take my arm to make me follow her—it was I who had to take hers, for she was crossing the avenue against the Don't Walk sign. It was the middle of the afternoon, with cars and cabs pounding down the street, but she ignored the angry shouts pursuing us. She was in a hurry to get me across and into the park to sit on a bench there. We walked past several before we found an empty one but had to move again because some children were playing ball too noisily nearby. Our next bench had some birds hopping around in front of it, and I thought she might move us again in search of the utter silence and solitude required for the reading of her daughter's poems. But finally she took them out and held them up again with that coy smile. Then she gave them to me. What could I say?

What can I say? I'm no judge of poetry, having spent my time reading and writing prose. In any case, the pages handed to me were hardly substantial enough to be matter for judgment. They were pages torn from a lined copy-book; the paper had turned somewhat brittle, but the ink was unfaded. Although the poems were written over several years—the date had been carefully inscribed in another hand at the top of each page—the handwriting never varied but remained clear and childlike. So did the poems. They were very, very simple, in thought and vocabulary. I would say that they were naive except that they were imbued with something that was not naive. Perhaps all the poems written by children are like that: lucid to the point of being translu-cent, so that the light of another world appears to shine through them. These looked as if they had all been written with the same fountain pen, probably an early birthday present.

They now belong to me, having been left to me by Helena when she died three years ago. There would have been no one else to take an interest in them. Dr. Manarr had died a year earlier, and Helena's ex-husband, Peter Koenig, the father of her daughter, had long ago had a fatal stroke brought on by high blood pressure. The children of his second marriage are still alive—as is their mother, whom they have placed in an expensive retirement home in New Jersey—but I don't think they would ever read this book, or perhaps any book; unlike Helena's daughter, they have taken completely after their father's side, so that both the family business and the family type are firmly established, and the first Koenig child can be seen as a deviation, a momentary aberration due to the Manarr strain.

After our first talk in the park, Helena persistently telephoned me—her calls became almost daily—wanting to meet me, to tell me some things and show me others. I often made excuses, which she brushed aside, so that I found myself visiting her in the various places she moved to. They were all, as I said, in the area where her daughter had lived—I believe one of them was even in the same building—and appeared to be almost identical. Impersonally functional and with no view, they were all dark and so musty that when you first entered you thought she kept some old animal in there; but it was she herself who was old and uncared for and lived shut up inside as in a lair. She flung everything open for me to see and know and remember. Among her own dusty dresses hung some flowered tea-gowns, which she said had belonged to her mother. One closet held her daughter's clothes and shoes from the age of twelve, and except that they varied in size, they seemed to be always the same: pleated skirts, and chesterfield coats with velvet collars, and flat-heeled shoes with laces or one strap across. When she showed me her many, many photographs of her daughter—these, too, are now mine—I saw that the girl herself did not change much over the years.

Helena pursued me because I was a writer, and she wanted her daughter's life story written. Unfortunately it was impossible to tell whether the daughter ever developed as a poet, for there was nothing beyond the juvenilia I had seen on the park bench. All the later work, according to Helena, was lost. It was always these same childish pages that Helena showed me over the three years—the last three of her life—that she hunted and haunted me; always the same facts she told me; the same photographs and books and clothes she showed me. There was nothing beyond them. And then toward the end I began to realize that this was what so tormented her—this silence, this blank, where her daughter had once been. Only on one occasion did she actually speak of it: this was when I had again asked her whether there was no writing of a later date, I didn't even mean poems, just anything, a diary entry, a letter, a note— something. "Not a word," Helena said. "Not even one last word for me." The way she said this drew me for a moment into the great emptiness in which she lived.

I have searched for all the clues I could find in the odd little collection of books her daughter left behind. She so rarely marked a page that whatever she did underline takes on a special significance. Such as this passage from a medieval text she had, which was *doubly* underlined, so that I was tempted to inscribe it on the title page:

*And this truly is what a perfect lover must always do,
utterly and entirely despoiling himself of himself for the
sake of the thing he loves; and that not only for a time but
everlastingly. This is the exercise of love, which no one can
know except he who feels it.*

But it is not for me to ascribe an epigraph to someone else's
life story. As it is, I feel I have taken too much liberty with
the material at my disposal. Only there was so little of it,
what else could I do? That was why I kept postponing the
writing of this narrative, always hoping that something
more might turn up, or that my questions would succeed in
turning another key to Helena's memory. That never happened, and, in fact, by the time I started writing, Helena
had died and there was no one left to tell me anything. But
then somewhere I came across a quotation—from Goethe,
I think it was—to the effect that the account of any life is
bound to be a mixture of fact and imagination; and for my
present purpose, I took this to mean that since Helena's
daughter had left so little of the former I was free to make
whatever use I could of the latter. And in another way, too,
I had no choice: having spent a lifetime writing fiction—
that is, making up characters and what they would say and
do in hypothetical situations—I found that, when I had to
tell something that really happened, I could do so only with
the same spurious methods I had always practiced.

   Here I was going to end my explanation of how I came
to write this memoir, but there is a postscript. Last year a
very aged aunt of mine who lives in England came to visit
me. Like the Manarr and Koenig families, my aunt came
originally from Germany, and every afternoon at four she

has to have her coffee and cake. While in New York she chose to have this in the hotel where Dr. Manarr's daughter had once lived—now greatly changed, and though still old-world, overflowing with gilded cupids and metalled fruits and blooms. My aunt is loquacious and vivacious and interested in everyone, so she routinely gets into conversation with waiters. On our second afternoon visit the waiter serving us turned out to be called Roland and was the same Roland who had worked there twenty-five years earlier, when Dr. Manarr's daughter had been a resident. He remembered her well, and her cousin, although he had no wish to talk about them at length. After my aunt returned to London, I sought him out again, and he agreed to meet me for a drink on his day off. He spoke more freely then, at least about himself and his adventures in the intervening years. He had only recently returned to work in the hotel; in between he had tried to better himself and had twice started a deli–restaurant of his own and twice failed, due to dark forces at work in the city. He hinted that there was much he could tell me about these, but finally all he said was that he was glad to be out of it and to have his old job again, even though at his age it was not easy on the feet and lower back.

I asked him about Angel and Lara. He still didn't have much to say about them—it was long ago, after all, and much had happened to him since. In the end I asked him outright if he thought that Lara had suffered from some form of schizophrenia or other severe personality disorder. He dismissed this quite contemptuously. "She wasn't mad," he said. "Just bad. People are, believe it or not," he added. "You can call it by all the fancy names you please, but that's what it is. There are good people trying to do all right, and there are bad ones that pull them down and win." I could see from the expression on his face that he was no longer answering my question, but speaking out of his own experience of living and working in the city.

IN HER EARLY years Angel had thought of herself as a poet. This was before she even knew it was possible to write words—in fact, it was better, for then there was nothing, no unwieldly medium, between her and her ecstatic soul. She simply uttered. Her first utterance came when she was three years old. By this time she and her mother had already left her father and gone to live with her grandparents, Anna and Siegfried Manarr. Every morning, while her mother was still asleep, Angel breakfasted with her grandparents. She sat on the carpet and fed pieces of roll to her doll. Above her Anna and Siegfried talked to her and to each other; she talked to them, to the doll, into space. And it was into space she said her first poem, which was two lines and involved a flower and a frog. Anna and Siegfried, whose attention with regard to Angel was absolute, heard her immediately. They looked at her, they looked at each other. Siegfried lifted her from the carpet—she grabbed her doll to go with her—and now she was sitting at the breakfast table. This was not in the dining but in the living room; it was a round table covered with a lace cloth, just by the window, so that the sun shone through the breakfast china, which was blue and gold. There were these smells: coffee, hot rolls, Siegfried's eau de cologne, Anna's heavy, warm perfume that breathed out of the deepest pores of her body. Angel sat on Siegfried's knee, and surrounded by their rosy, smiling faces, she repeated her poem. They kissed—first her, then each other; so she said her poem again, louder and bolder, and then again. Each time they were more astonished, so that she couldn't say it enough and also tried variations, while they wondered and marveled: with such a reaction, it was only natural for Angel to consider herself, and to be considered, a poet.

Later she recognized that this memory of her first poem, along with the rest of her early impressions, was idealized. For one thing, no one's grandparents, no human beings, could live in such perfect happiness as Anna and Siegfried. They worshiped each other, along with Angel and her mother, Helena. The four of them lived in a brownstone, which was quite narrow but had several stories and a basement leading into a little garden with a stone nymph holding a bird. It adjoined other gardens, most of them paved but with some trees and flowers planted in tubs or boxes. It was part of Angel's idealized vision that their row of brownstones was on a quiet street surrounded by other quiet streets, and with no huge buildings or roaring avenues around them. Yet they lived in the middle of the city, and even then there must have been some of the great blocks of apartment and office buildings that now hemmed them in entirely. Angel's earliest impressions were summed up not in a poem but a drawing that her mother had kept: it showed one house, one tree, and standing next to these and bigger than either, two people—Anna and Siegfried—with round stomachs and round buttons all the way down.

Anna and Siegfried both came from Germany. They had met at a spa where Siegfried had gone for his summer vacation. He had already entered the family firm—he was a businessman, but idealistic, romantic, and shyly looking for a bride. Anna was eighteen, virginal, in first bloom—a large bloom even then, soft and voluptuous, but her big body balanced on slender legs. Love made Siegfried bold: in the hotel dining room he dared to look often to the table where Anna sat between her parents, her eyes never raised from her plate but her cheeks growing warm under the rays of Siegfried's gaze. More prosaic forces than their own delicately unfolding desires propelled them. Anna's family business had connections in New York, Siegfried's was establishing them, and he was to be sent as their principal representative. He spoke good English, having as a child been tutored by an English miss, and also had a good personality: he genuinely liked people, he shook their hands warmly, knowing them to be as honest as himself. Before he had admitted his feelings to Anna, and before she had had time to admit hers to herself, their families were arranging their wedding. So it happened that their courtship was cut short, which was perhaps the reason they spent the rest of their lives making up for it.

Every working day Siegfried left for an office and Anna saw him off, helping him into his coat. He was punctual and punctilious about attendance, though it was not known exactly what he did when he got there. Whenever he or Anna mentioned "the business" they made a respectful, even solemn face; this was probably to compensate for their entire lack of interest in it. Both of them lived only for the moment when he came home again in the evening; Anna watched out for him from an upstairs window. On rainy days they had a fire lit and sat by it playing chemin de fer; on fine days their car came around and they sat holding hands in the backseat and were driven through the park. They had many cultural interests and went to art exhibitions and plays, having read the review aloud to one another and afterward comparing their own impressions with it. They usually agreed with the reviewer and they always agreed with each other. They were two separate large, plump bodies, but in everything else they were one. Their principal interest was music, and during the season they were at the opera every Wednesday and at a concert of chamber music on Sunday afternoons. One day they decided that Siegfried would take singing lessons and engaged a teacher for him—a musical genius, for it was the time when there were many talented refugees eager to make a living. Siegfried stood by the piano with one hand laid on it; the teacher—tiny, balding with a tuft of long hair growing from each temple—crouched on the piano stool raised as high as for a child; and Anna watched from the couch with a smile on her face and a handkerchief crushed in her hand to contain her emotion. She couldn't understand why the teacher wouldn't let Siegfried proceed from the first song, nor indeed from the first bars of the first song, which he made him repeat over and over. The teacher banged and shouted and seemed sometimes to weep, but Siegfried remained calm, smiling at this display of artistic temperament. He was amazed when one day his teacher slammed the piano lid shut and, clutching at his tufts of hair, left the house never to return. Anna wanted to engage another teacher—a more sympathetic one even if not a genius—but Siegfried dissuaded her, gently accepting his fate of having no talent. From then on they looked eagerly toward their two children, Helena and Hugo, but it turned out that they, too, had no musical talent.

YET IT WAS time for the family to throw up some artistic potential. They had prospered in business for almost 150 years; earlier generations had been content to make money, lead good bourgeois lives, and make more money; later ones developed other, mainly cultural interests, although these were always in second place to their business affairs. It was not until Siegfried and Anna that this order was reversed; but then their children seemed to reverse it again. Helena showed an early ability to make money. She derived an income from the family business but took no part in it; instead, she started her own—when she was still at college she went into partnership with another student who made jewelry and successfully sold it for her. Later she took up with some people who designed lingerie and soon ran several high-class boutiques. Hugo went away to medical school and got married and was not seen much at home during those years—that is, the first years that Angel could remember. For her, these were filled entirely by her grand-parents and by her mother. Although it was Anna and Sieg-fried who were there to hear her first poem, it was Helena who inspired it, if it is true that one's artistic achievements are inspired by the deepest passion of the heart.

In later years Helena became, like Anna, big and over-weight, though without her mother's phlegmatic disposi-tion. Even in youth she had been physically solid with broad cheekbones and broad hips; her hair was dark and heavy and she wore it hanging down her back with bangs cut straight across her forehead. She was full of energy and had a loud voice and tramped up and down the stairs. When she was home, the little brownstone—full enough already with her two large parents—bulged with her pres-ence; but she was often out, and then Angel spent her time waiting for her to return. When Angel was ill, Helena stayed home, and this may have been why Angel was often ill. The essence of Angel's early childhood was lying in bed with a very high temperature—in her mother's bed, which she appropriated for the occasion. She watched Helena move around the room and felt her fever rise and burn inside her.

Angel went to school in the same way as Siegfried went to the office—dutifully, respectfully, and waiting for the moment when she could return home. Only her time at home really counted, so it was intolerable to have to give up any of it; for instance, to her paternal grandmother, who sometimes asked to see her. When this happened, and Angel failed to manage a fever, Helena had to coax her from the moment of waking and also call for Siegfried and Anna to do the same. Angel knew very well that it was not possible for Helena to accompany her on these visits, but right till the last minute she pretended to think it was. When the cab delivered them outside the apartment house, Angel wouldn't get out but clung to Helena and had to be disengaged amid pleading and promises and then handed over to the doorman who stood waiting to lead her away.

By the time she arrived upstairs, having been handed from doorman to elevator man, Angel had resigned herself. She had even, remembering Helena's admonitions, made some good resolutions, such as not to cry and not to ask to be taken home. And her grandmother Koenig had also made good resolutions—she wore a smile on her chronically unsmiling face and held Angel to her midriff, although releasing her almost at once to smooth her dress where Angel's face had touched it. Angel was used to large grandparents, but whereas Anna and Siegfried softly surrounded her, Grandmother Koenig towered above her—dark in her plum-colored crepe and her pinnacle of hair brushed into a silver pompadour. And it was not only she who towered but her whole enormous apartment thickly populated with furniture, and chandeliers hanging down, mostly in dust shrouds, though in the rooms in use they had to be kept on all day because the natural light was blocked by the surrounding buildings.

Grandmother Koenig, having made inquiries as to Angel's favorite dishes, had had her maid prepare them. This maid, Lina, who had been with Grandmother Koenig since her marriage and was no longer on speaking terms with her, had her own style of cuisine, which was heavy and glutinous and extremely difficult for Angel to swallow. Nevertheless, still full of good resolutions, she managed to push some morsels down her throat; Grandmother Koenig was also keeping up her end, telling Angel about the dinner parties they used to have at this very table where now only the two of them were—twenty sitting down, she said, all of them Grandfather Koenig's business colleagues and their wives, eating five-course meals with a different wine for each course. The food Angel had forced down sat on her stomach in a lump, but still she swallowed more; the silverware was as heavy as gold, the edges and center circles of the plates really were gold; Lina banged in and out of the kitchen, furious but efficient. Sitting bolt upright under her pompadour, Grandmother Koenig spoke of the tremendous responsibility of these dinner parties, which had rested entirely on her shoulders—the menu, the flowers, the seating and table arrangements—"What is the matter, Angelica?" For the momentous struggle not to spit her food out, not to throw up, had flushed and swelled Angel's face, tears were in her eyes—and then gushed out when she was called by the name of Angelica: she who was Angel, Helena's Angel, and where *was* Helena? Now she had to spit out on to her golden plate, the lump on her stomach rose, she swallowed it back, she choked: abandoned in misery, her condition was made worse by the expression she saw on Grandmother Koenig's face—it was not so much anger as the disappointment of someone who had done her utmost and failed.

GRANDMOTHER KOENIG'S SON Peter—who was Angel's father—said not to send Angel there anymore, what was the use? Attempts to make Angel visit his own house—he was remarried and had three small sons—had been mostly abandoned, so he had to come and see her at home. Although she liked his visits, she found that they did not have a good effect on Helena. He regularly showed up whenever Angel was sick, which was also at regular intervals. Everyone tried hard, no one wished to upset Angel. Actually, Peter should have had a soothing influence. He was cheerful and kind, and his manly hand was cool on Angel's hot brow. Nevertheless she shut her eyes in the hope that he would go away soon. But he lingered. He asked about this and that, all concerning Angel, and included questions that had already been asked and answered. He stood by the window, rattling his keys against coins in his pocket. Helena had her back to him, fixing her hair in the mirror in which she could also see his reflection. Soon they would begin to disagree. It might start off with Angel's visits to Grandmother Koenig—which Peter himself not ten minutes before had said were not necessary, and yet now he suggested that Angel should go there more often. Helena turned around from the mirror, her half-done hair swung angrily, she said did he have any idea what it cost her to get the child there at all? Peter said that's what he meant: they should become more used to each other, perhaps go on outings together—afternoon tea in the Palm Court, to the zoo—Helena shouted, "Your mother and Angel to the *zoo!*" Angel herself, lying in bed with her eyes shut, was not in the least disturbed. She knew that Peter didn't mean what he said, he was talking only because he didn't want to leave. He shrugged away his own suggestion —it didn't have to be the zoo—and Helena, continuing to fix her hair, said, "Then why do you say these things?" Peter replied that surely it was natural for him to take an

interest in his daughter's visits to his mother—he pretended
to be aggrieved but actually sounded satisfied, to have provoked her into an argument. Then both he and Angel
waited for Helena to say: "You've got other children, why
don't you send them?" And when she had said it, Peter cast
a warning look toward Angel—who shut her eyes so tight,
anyone would know she was awake and listening; and he
stepped closer to Helena to murmur: "But Angel was the
first." Perhaps he spoke only for the sake of thus standing
and remaining very close to Helena, who did not move
away. Their proximity lasted only moments; but it was a
matter not so much of time present as of a past that had
once been theirs in common and could not be wiped out
any more than Angel herself. It was always Helena who
moved away, toward the bed, saying, "I'll call you, I'll tell
you how she is." "First thing in the morning," Peter said.
"In the office." He, too, came toward the bed, and they
stood on either side of it; and at the same moment each put
out a hand to feel Angel's forehead, and when they
touched, Peter laughed and said "Sorry," and then it was
only his hand that stroked her forehead and hair while Helena stood waiting for him to leave.

DURING THOSE YEARS Hugo lived partly in Eu-
rope and partly on the West Coast, and his infrequent visits
brought much excitement to his parents and sister. They all
wanted to get him on his own—even Anna and Siegfried
had separate secret confabulations with him, in which, it
turned out, each wanted to be reassured about the other's
health. They called him the Herr Doktor, though he had

already stopped practicing medicine and was getting involved in various forms of experimental psychiatry. His parents didn't understand what it was he was doing but they had tremendous faith in his cleverness. "He has it up here," said Siegfried, tapping his own forehead, which was high and nobly arched but gave the impression of a certain hollowness due to lack of experience, or innocence. Anna, too, was very simple. Hugo did not say anything clever to anyone—in fact, he said little, and when he did tried to make it into a joke, as though afraid of getting into those serious waters that were his professional habitat. He had an air of laziness—perhaps he *was* lazy—with his long body mostly in a state of relaxation. He half lay in an easy chair, letting his limbs dangle. He amused Angel with letting her swing his hand, hanging limp from his wrist as if about to drop off.

On one of his visits he arranged to have his parents photographed. A woman photographer arrived, another German refugee, very old, famous, and bad-tempered. She strode all over the house, and deciding to use their living room, had them move the furniture around till the big flowered couch was center stage. She arranged Anna and Siegfried on it side by side exactly how they always sat there: but she posed them in such a way that their togetherness took on a sort of eternal, archetypal quality. She worked like a demon, muttering to herself in street-smart German and snapping at Anna and Siegfried in the same German not to fidget. Helena and Hugo were sent off on continuous errands, such as getting Siegfried's spats for him to wear and another pair of her little stud earrings for Anna. All this took a long time, and everyone's excitement turned

into boredom, which Hugo tried to relieve by making faces
at his parents behind the photographer's back. To suppress
her giggles, Anna made an oversolemn face, tucking in her
chin so that it developed one more fold above her string of
pearls.

On the nights when Hugo and Helena went out to see
a film or listen to jazz musicians, Angel slept in her grandparents' bedroom between the two of them in their double
bed on their high spring mattress. They lay on their backs,
each an identical size mound under the covering, and were
very soon asleep. They always kept a night-light on so that
the familiar room—orderly, fragrant, flowers on the curtains, flowers on the pastel carpet—was clearly visible to
Angel, who stayed awake much longer. She wriggled between them, but their sleep remained undisturbed; they
breathed as they did everything, in unison. Angel dropped
off but woke at once when she heard the voices from the
room above that she had been waiting for even in her sleep.
She slipped out between her grandparents and crept up to
Helena's room. Hugo was stretched out on the chaise
longue at the foot of his sister's bed; he wore striped pajamas that made him look longer and thinner than ever. They
still hadn't finished talking; there was an air of melancholy
as though both spoke of disappointment, or unfulfillment.
Angel got in with Helena and lay against her and went to
sleep again. When she woke, Hugo was gone and was not
seen till he came down at noon, yawning in his pajamas. He
made out to be so tired that he stretched out again on the
sofa and shut his eyes and let his mother feed him his breakfast morsel by morsel. Every now and again he bit her

finger to make her laugh, catching hold of it with his teeth and not letting go.

HUGO WAS MARRIED but he never brought his wife. Usually she was somewhere far away, like Iran or India, or she was sick. He didn't speak of her much except maybe in those long talks he and Helena had alone together at night. There was a daughter, Lara, whom Angel longed to meet, but it was not until she herself was eight and Lara seven that Hugo brought her on one of his visits. Here it must be admitted that Angel, though the jewel in the lotus of that household, was not pretty. She already wore glasses, and it was obvious that soon she would need braces on her teeth. The cute dresses that were bought for her did not become her. Of course no one noticed her plainness except Grandmother Koenig. And probably Angel herself was the only one in the house who was conscious of the contrast she presented to her cousin. For Lara was very pretty, and knew it, and also knew the attendant obligation to be charming. She fully accepted it. She kissed her relatives with her lips thrust far forward to show how much pleasure this gave her. Arranging her dress daintily, she sat facing her grandparents, who were side by side as usual with Angel between them. She showed herself ready to answer any questions they might put to her; and when they appeared too shy to begin, she herself volunteered all the information anyone might want to know about her—her age, her attitude to animals, her favorite foods and those she couldn't stand—she prattled freely, pleased to astonish and delight.

Only Hugo, entering upon this charmed circle, suggested she shouldn't be talking so much. She cast an injured look not at him but at her audience—who justified her at once by begging her to continue. But her mood was changed, and instead of lavishing herself on all three, she now concentrated on Angel, and her head laid a little bit to one side, she invited her: "Shall we play?" with enchanting formality.

Angel wanted to give her cousin everything she possessed. She threw open her closet and dresser for her, but although Lara politely admired the contents, she did not desire anything except Angel's pearl brooch, which her grandparents had given her on her last birthday. This she accepted more to please Angel than herself, shutting it into her little purse to carry off as a memento of Angel.

It was their grandparents who suggested that Angel should recite her poems to her cousin. As soon as she began, she found that in Lara's presence a multitude of new poems that she hadn't even known about came to her— flowed out of her—on every conceivable topic. She went on and on, and the grandparents listened, nudging each other and Helena listened. Hugo leaned forward—he looked at Helena in surprise—he tried to make Angel repeat some of her poems but she couldn't remember what she had said: each poem, each bird, flower, cloud, star, lake, and person, each one was every time new. Lara sat with her feet in patent leather shoes crossed at the ankles, and she smiled all the way through the recital to show she was enjoying it. At last she said, "Shall I do my dance?" Hugo said, "What dance?" and then "Let's hear Angel's poems." But before these words were out of his mouth, Angel was begging Lara for her dance and sat down at once between her grandparents to watch her.

Lara threw herself into her performance. To help her audience, she called out, "Now I am a flower!" "Now a princess!" "See the deer!" Although her movements were always the same—she waved her arms above her head, she ran now to the right of the room, now to the left—her audience obligingly saw what she wanted them to see. She was pleased, she ran faster, she attempted to spin around; her tread was not light, and she was flustered and breathing hard, but every time Hugo said "That's enough, Lara," she started up again with renewed energy and desperate invention—"A fish swimming in the sea! A magic fish!"—until she herself decided: "That's the end," and stood before them, holding the edge of her pleated skirt, curtsying, and drinking up their applause, radiance streaming from her face, her eyes brilliant with self-pleasure.

That night in bed she told Angel, "When I grow up, I'm going to be a dancer." They slept in the same room, so that for the first time in her life Angel did not find it necessary, not once through the whole night, to go in to her mother. "I'll be a dancer," Lara said, "and you can be a poet. . . . You want to come in my bed?" When Angel hesitated, she complained, "I'm cold." Angel's hesitation had been due to shyness, and even fear, like fearing to want something too much; but now she went over to the other bed, which had been brought into her room for Lara, and slipped under the cover held open for her. Lara folded it around the two of them; she snuggled up close and whispered, "Feel how cold I am." She guided Angel's hand; she wasn't cold at all but exuded heat from under the gown which she pushed up to allow Angel to feel her. Guiding her hand farther down, she held on to it when she felt a movement as of withdrawal—but if Angel held back, it was again out of that same fear. "Do you like it?" Lara whispered, squeezing Angel's hand between her thighs. Their hearts were beating together under the bedclothes. Lara was twitching, and clinging to Angel, and her own hand was now between Angel's thighs, introducing there the strangest sensation. "Go on—like I'm doing," she instructed Angel, her heart beating faster, her thighs squeezing tighter, a muscle throbbing there more urgently; her mouth was wide open, her breath blew hot in Angel's face; she was emitting some strange sound. Quite abruptly all that activity stopped and she rolled away. Angel was left in a deprivation that was the physical equivalent of what she felt at Grandmother Koenig's table when suddenly overwhelmed by the absence of Helena. But only for a moment—because whatever strange sensation might have gotten hold of Angel, its cessation was of no importance compared with the fact that Lara was still there beside her. Moreover, Lara said, "You can stay with me, but don't *move*"—which Angel took so literally that she tried to keep awake all night for fear of moving in her sleep.

THEY DIDN'T MEET again till they were grown-up. Angel and her mother continued to live in the little brownstone, but most of the other houses in their row had been sold and subdivided into apartments. Of those that remained, one was under legal dispute, and in the other a famous movie star lived out her years of neglect and old age. Similar houses in neighboring streets had been replaced by thirty-story apartment buildings. New supermarkets had opened at every corner, and supplementing them all along the streets and avenues were Italian fruit and vegetable markets, Greek-owned delis, cigarette and stationery stores, takeout barbecued chicken places, and Chinese laundries.

Anna and Siegfried had died—very quickly and in quick succession to each other. Siegfried had gone first, and while Angel remembered visiting him in his hospital room and throwing earth into his grave, she had no recollection of any protracted illness. When he was gone there was a dramatic change in Anna left behind. She put aside her floral silks and wore what appeared to be always the same musty black dress; and deserting her marital bedroom, she lived down in the basement with the curtains drawn against the garden and any light that might come in. This did not last long, and after another hospital room and grave, she, too, was gone.

But now Helena changed, and so radically that it was difficult to resurrect the memory of the earlier Helena. She could not accept the death of her parents. In her mourning she became like Anna in hers—wore only the one black dress and stayed down in the basement with the curtains drawn. She left her business to subordinates, and when they ruined it, she remained inert, indifferent; she didn't want to start anything up again. Angel looked after her. She ran the house for both of them, arranging the basement so that Helena could move down there permanently. These were busy years for Angel, for she also attended school and passed a lot of exams and went on to college; but her main work was always at home, with Helena. When Peter, her father, protested she was doing too much, she assured him that she could easily manage; and this was true, for in spite of all those childhood illnesses, Angel grew up sturdily. Unlike the rest of her family on both sides, she wasn't tall but she was strong, stocky, with muscular calves and broad shoulders. There was nothing ethereal about her appearance, nor angelic, except for her hair, which sat on her head in a cap of thick tight curls. Her eyes were light blue; when she mislaid her glasses, her gaze was dreamy due to nearsightedness.

She had ceased to write poetry; she had too many practical concerns that seemed to shut a door between her and whatever it was that had made her write the poetry. Mostly she forgot about it, and if sometimes she felt some stir in that region, she tried to ignore it because she felt that if she opened the door or opened herself to what lay behind it, then there would be no space or time for all the rest.

IN ANGEL'S SENIOR year of college, Helena began to revive. She still had one boutique—all the others had been closed—and it was through this that she met Mrs. Arora, an Indian lady who imported fine embroideries stitched by orphan girls in Indian convents. Helena's remaining store was one of her outlets, and she adopted Helena and Angel as her friends. She cooked Indian dishes for them and brought them herself or sent them with her son, Rohit, who worked in an airlines office. Gliding in her sari, she seemed not so much to enter a room as to insinuate herself into it; the same was true of her manner of establishing relationships, which slid subtly over the dividing line between acquaintance and intimacy. She had a soft voice which she never raised but frequently lowered in sympathy for someone else's suffering. Her hands were hot, and she was always ready to massage away a headache. There was even a suspicion that her touch held some special healing power, though she herself did not make this claim any more than she claimed unusual psychological penetration; yet she appeared very quickly to sense a mood or state of feeling, offering her perfect understanding of it.

From their first contact through the orphans' embroideries, she treated Helena, who hadn't made a new acquaintance in years, as a family member. Carrying her little Indian dishes under a lace cloth, she descended to Helena's retreat in the basement and stayed with her for many hours. She encouraged her to speak of her parents, her former joy in them, her present grief. After a while she put her hand on the drawn curtain—"May I?"—and opened it. Light came in from the garden and fell on Helena. Mrs. Arora continued to listen with full sympathy, very gently flicking off the specks of dust that the sunlight showed up on Helena's dark dress. Then she stroked her hair, first in a gesture of sympathy, then to admire, for it was long and thick though also thickly streaked with gray. She suggested some other way of fixing it, for Helena still wore it hanging down her back as she had done as a girl. Mrs. Arora offered, and in the end prevailed, to wash and set it. She did so playfully but also proved very adept, and Helena's neglected hair was piled into a shining shampooed coil—still gray, for Helena resisted the very special Indian dye her friend offered her from her private stock. Mrs. Arora's own hair sat on her head in terraced, lacquered layers of deepest black.

Angel became best friends with Rohit. It started almost from his first visit, when he came bearing one of his mother's dishes. He appeared to be very shy, but when he realized that Angel was even more shy, he manfully took charge. He opened up the dishes, explained what they were, and insisted that she should taste some, though it was ten o'clock in the morning and hardly the time for a lamb curry. He served her himself, and not to be outdone in politeness, she sat and ate. He watched her with concern— "It's not too hot for you?" She said no. He explained the ingredients, and with mounting enthusiasm how the spices were to be pounded and fried—"first the onions, then add cumin—only this much—ginger, garlic—it *is* too hot for you!" Angel coughed: "I only need some water—I always drink a lot of water when I eat." He got it for her, she gulped it down to relieve her burning palate, and was at once ready to continue eating. He wouldn't let her, though she insisted she liked it, loved it—they were tugging at the plate, both protesting. This became the epitome of their relationship: a concern to spare each other's feelings, to give only pleasure and to spare from pain.

Angel began often to visit the apartment where Rohit lived with his mother. It was only two streets away, in one of the gigantic buildings that had gone up in the past few years. It had a garish lobby with orange-tinted walls and lighting, and was crammed with the tiniest apartments possible. The Aroras had two rooms which were hardly big enough for a single average-size one, but they managed very well. One bed and a prayer corner took up all of the room where the mother slept, and their tiny living room held a sofa, which converted into Rohit's bed at night, some carved furniture imported from India, along with a gold statue of a god, and a Kashmiri carpet that was too big for the floor so that it stuck up against the baseboard. Incense burned before the idol in the bedroom as well as before the golden god. The smell of frying spices penetrated the apartment and sometimes reached right into the elevator. There seemed to be frequent visitors from India stowed away in this small space, but their presence was not easy to detect—only sometimes someone coughed in the bedroom, or a figure came shuffling out to use the bathroom and was easily explained as "It's only Uncle."

Mrs. Arora and Helena went into partnership, and the boutique flourished. They could have opened some others but chose instead to supply their imports to the best stores in the country, Mrs. Arora establishing excellent relationships with their leading buyers. The basement of the brownstone was used as an office, and Helena moved back upstairs, now taking over her parents' bedroom. They had many orders to deal with, as well as bureaucratic business such as import licenses, and would have had to engage clerical help but for Angel, who had just graduated and took up that job. For the sake of making contacts, Mrs. Arora gave more ambitious entertainments for which her apartment was too small, so the living rooms of the brownstone were opened up, along with the cabinets and sideboards crammed to overflowing with Siegfried and Anna's tea and dinner and dessert and fruit services and glasses for every kind of wine and liqueur. Mrs. Arora cooked in the kitchen, and the smells crept all over the house and incense was lit to disguise them, so that although the house itself and all its furnishings were as they had been, the ambience began to resemble that of the Arora apartment.

"Who *are* these people?" Peter asked about the Aroras. He was suspicious of them from the first and also objected to Angel turning herself into what he called their clerk; it was not, he said, what he had paid college tuition for. He had been proud of Angel's doing well—though not very well—at school, unlike his boys, who found it very difficult to graduate. He would have liked Angel to study more, qualify as something or other, he said. But what she was doing suited her because it kept her at home, both literally and in another way. It seemed to her that any going out into the world was a scattering of her senses, and of some store of inward resources she wanted to keep intact.

Angel had continued her visits to Grandmother Koenig, and they had become voluntary. Both of them were rewarded for persisting in a difficult relationship, so that it had become strong between them, if not always pleasant. There was much—one might even say everything—about Angel that her grandmother deplored, yet she prepared carefully for her arrival and sat by a window to watch out for it. Her maid Lina, by this time totally deaf, was still with her and still cooked the same meals, but now Angel had no difficulty swallowing them. They sat at the long table where the Koenig dinner parties had been enacted in former days, and Grandmother Koenig voiced all her complaints—about her doctor, who didn't know how to relieve the pain in her knee, about Lina, about the quality of the meat sold by the butcher, about her other grandchildren, who were too busy to come and see her. This took them past the fruit salad

which was Lina's only known dessert—at the dinner parties, when there had still been a proper cook in the house,
an elaborate ice bombe was often served—and then they
went to the drawing room, which was kept immaculate,
ready for use though not encouraging it. By this time
Grandmother Koenig had passed from the grandchildren to
their mother, Lilian, Peter's second wife, who was responsible for their lack of affection and manners. Grandmother
Koenig, although now very old, was still very upright, and
when she spoke with indignation, her coiffure seemed to
grow taller. Her face took on an expression of scorn, di-
rected in the first place at her absent daughter-in-law, and
then redirected at Lina, who entered with the coffee tray
clattering in her old hands. *"Instant* coffee, no doubt,"
sneered Grandmother Koenig, but since Lina's deafness
made her impervious, it was Angel who had to bear the
brunt. From this point on her good humor with Angel and
good resolutions with regard to herself went downhill. She
inquired about Angel's spectacles and why she wore them
when everyone else had contact lenses; she mentioned that
she considered high heels more becoming than the flat loaf-
ers in which Angel walked about. She passed on to Angel's
progress and prospects; she believed in speaking her mind
but, as she spoke it, looked as displeased with herself as with
her granddaughter. At last, "Get me my tablets," she said,
and Angel hurried to obey, for she knew that Grandmother
Koenig had dyspepsia after her meals, and this partly ac-
counted for the ill humor that clouded the close of each
visit.

.   .   .

IN THE MEANTIME Hugo had become famous. Af-
ter several years with experimental groups in California, he
moved first to Paris, to work with an avant-garde analyst
there, then to Edinburgh, to qualify in more traditional
methods. Based on these experiences, he published a book
expounding a new approach to problems of the psyche,
which became very influential in popular more than in aca-
demic circles. He was in demand as a lecturer, and there
were several centers in Europe and the U.S. where groups
conducted self-experiments based on his methods. He traveled extensively, and at first enjoyed it; he was quite free,
for by this time his marriage had broken up. Lara was in
boarding schools, which she changed often, either because
her mother took her away or she decided to leave on her
own. In her last year at a school in England her mother died
suddenly of an overdose of a drug she had been using habit-
ually for some time. To give Lara a home base, Hugo decided to settle in New York and took a large apartment
there; but Lara stayed behind in England—to study, her
father said, though he wasn't sure what.

Hugo was not lonely. Many women took an interest in
him, and avoiding the very high-strung ones his work
tended to attract, he formed relationships with married
women who were motherly and pampered him. His sister
Helena was very happy to have him back again. She was
proud of his fame and read his books—there were several by
then—but if she tried to talk to him about them, he turned
the subject aside, usually with a joke. When she wanted to
join one of his groups, he told her to go to a weight-loss
one instead. He had been startled by the change in her
appearance, and in the beginning kept looking at her as

though trying to pick out the former Helena from among the mass that now embedded her.

Angel, too, had read his books, and while she, too, was proud of his fame, the theory on which his work was based repelled her. Of course she never admitted this to anyone, not even to her mother, and when his books were mentioned, she always had some sentences of neutral praise, such as about his style. She was relieved that he himself never cared to discuss his work with his family. Once or twice he asked her about her poetry; she said she never wrote any. This was a lie, for she had started again, but in what was an almost neurotic secrecy. He said, "That's a pity, you used to be good." "Yes, at five years old," Angel smiled. He agreed that children were able to express themselves with a directness that was no longer possible for them as adults; although, he added, it could be induced again by means of certain exercises—well, he wouldn't go into any of that now. She knew these exercises were part of his method and was grateful he didn't urge them on her. She didn't know what they did for other people, but for herself she feared them: that is, for her poetry, insofar as she had any to write.

Angel's room was now on the top story. It was narrow and rectangular, and on one wall were her books—not very many, for she discarded them once they had, as she put it to herself, entered her bloodstream. On the opposite wall was a bed and a reproduction of a dim, shy, mild Madonna she had liked and bought in a museum. Inside the window stood a table and chair from where she looked up at the surrounding apartment buildings. At night, points of light swarmed up their sides, like stars scattered over a range of dark mountains. Angel did her work with the import business in the basement office, and when she came upstairs she sat at this table and tried to write poetry. It came very hard. When she was small, words had flown out of her like birds; now they fell back into her like stones. Their hardness seemed to lacerate her, and often she had to rest her head on the table to recover before she could go on. Mostly she did go on, and afterward she hid the loose papers inside her table drawer, dreading the moment when she would have to take them out again and yet also obscurely waiting for it the rest of the time. She discarded many pages and had matches for burning them in the fireplace, which was used for no other purpose.

The only person who knew about her writing was Rohit. She had confided in him because he himself was so entirely open with her—that was what friendship meant for him, confiding one's secrets to another person. Apart from her writing, however, Angel had no secrets and that was why she felt she owed him at least this one. His own secrets were more easily told: his unrequited passion for an airline hostess; his difficulties in learning new languages. There were also bouts of homesickness. "Please don't think I'm not happy here, Angel. I have so much! Mummy is here, and mostly my job is quite nice, and you're here. It's only sometimes—well, you know—I think of our place at home, and playing with my dog. We had a German shepherd called Sultan, he waited for me by the gate to come home from school and then he went completely mad. He ran around in circles and bit his tail. . . . And then there's something else." His smile for his dog gave way to another expression. "I won't tell you today, but I will, another day."

      LARA CAME TO New York. It was fifteen years since she had been there, but Angel remembered every detail of her visit. Lara herself seemed to remember nothing—she said to Angel, "We did meet, didn't we, when I was here? Yes, of course we did," she said, smiling brilliantly at Angel, as though she had the fondest recollection of their meeting. She looked at Siegfried and Anna's prominently displayed portrait—the one taken by the German woman photographer—and she asked who they were. She said, "What a pity I never met them." Helena said, "Of course you met them," and Lara said at once, "Yes, but that was much later, wasn't it. . . . I love your house, Helena, who'd have thought to find such an adorable little place in the middle of Manhattan—oh, there's even a garden! Can I go out and see?" She went out, full of admiration, desiring to please rather than be pleased.

    Lara had come to live in New York because everywhere else had proved unsatisfactory. She had tried to develop her talent in other places and had worked with teachers who were good but not good for her because of a lack of communication at a deeper level. This she hoped to find here, where she had heard of people doing new and exciting work. "You mean in dance?" Angel said. "Dance, or whatever." "You were going to be a dancer," Angel said, smiling: she waited for Lara to say, "And you a poet." But Lara didn't seem to remember that either, and she went on,

"I've always loved dance but I'm beginning to wonder if it isn't a bit limited—limiting? At least for me." She seriously ruminated for a while, her cheek propped on her hand, and Angel watched her and waited for her to share her thoughts. But she suddenly shook them off: quite literally, by shaking back her hair in a gesture that had been characteristic of Helena when she was young—Lara's hair too was long but it was fair, bright gold—and she said, "Why are we talking only about me when you haven't told me one thing about you." Angel blushed; she was ready to tell whatever there was, but it was time for Lara to go—she had an appointment downtown, she was serious about getting going in her career.

She lived with her father in his apartment overlooking the park. There was plenty of room, but it was not the best arrangement for either of them. Hugo led a mixture of professional and bachelor life. Patients came to see him during certain hours in the week, and although there was a separate waiting room for them, they did have to cross the entrance hall, where Lara sometimes encountered them. When this happened she haughtily turned her face, irritated to think that they might mistake her for another patient. It was worse when she met one of his girlfriends, who were in the habit of freely moving around his apartment even when he was not there. They were always doing something for him—one of them had picked up an Uzbek carpet he had bought at an auction and had forgotten about, another came to hang some Daumier cartoons she had helped him find. Each vaguely knew about the others' relationship with Hugo though unsure how far it went, wondering, "Did she come only to hang the pictures?" But they all realized that Hugo needed many things done for him, and anyway, they were all more or less happily married, also tolerant, realistic, full of practical common sense —which was how Hugo needed his friends to be in contrast to his patients.

But his daughter was not in the least like that. This was what happened the first time she met one of these girlfriends: it was the one with the Uzbek carpet, she was kneeling on the floor, rolling it out. "Were you looking for someone?" said Lara, standing above her, and her stern expression did not change when the other winningly smiled up at her. The girlfriend began to explain about the carpet, and how helpless Hugo was and how they all spoiled him and made him more helpless. Lara cut her short—"I'm Dr. Manarr's daughter"—in a tone so forbidding that the other had quickly to finish unrolling the carpet, crawling away with it along the floor.

Hugo told his sister about his daughter: "When I see her from this side she's like you, and from the other she's Alice." Helena had never known Alice, Lara's mother, for Hugo's marriage had played itself out in distant places; but she knew that it had been difficult and disturbed and had ended long before Alice's death. It was a chapter that Hugo, with his need to remove himself from all unpleasantness, did his best to regard as closed, and he would probably have succeeded almost totally if it hadn't been for Lara. What he tried to tell Helena was that he loved the side of his daughter that recalled his sister—he had never known anyone except the two of them who moved in that particular way: planting their feet heavily on the ground to bear the full weight of their luxurious bodies, and yet appearing light, or, rather, buoyant. "Even now," he told Helena, "though you're so overluxurious: I can still tell it's you, anywhere." But Lara had her mother's very fine features— "no, not ours," he said, drawing his finger along his own strong nose and referring to his sister's similar one. Lara's was a profile brought to its present state of delicacy by continuous reproduction from the same seed in the same soil: for Lara's maternal family had been American for generations, and while never particularly distinguished or prominent, they had been proud of marrying only each other and continuing to live in their family homesteads even when these were falling about their ears.

"Can she dance or act or whatever it is she's doing?" Helena asked.

Hugo said, "It would be awful if she couldn't." Failure was something he had already gone through with Alice— that was her given name, though she had assumed others, according to whatever she was immersed in at the moment: Maya, Mira (for God-intoxication), at one stage Sister Clara. Unlike Lara, she had no artistic inclinations, but her goal was a higher consciousness, and she went to all sorts of places and all sorts of lengths to attain it.

Lara had accompanied her mother on some of these excursions or pilgrimages. When she was very small she had been happy to be dressed up in beads and to fold her hands before idols; on her own initiative she had brought offerings of marigolds in her tiny cupped hands. In later years, when she was at boarding schools in England or Switzerland and her mother appeared in the middle of the term to take her away, Lara was glad to go: she never liked any school she was in, she felt unappreciated. But the older she grew, the less she cared for the atmosphere in these holy places. They were usually situated in some dust bowl, and the devotees, even those radiant with an inner light, all suffered from amoebic dysentery. Plagued by mosquitoes, they lived in cement huts grouped around a brand-new palace built of colored bathroom tiles with a throne at its center, where some fat holy man oozed a honeyed mixture of religiosity and sexuality.

"OH, THAT *SMELL!* I can't bear it!" Lara exclaimed. She meant the incense Mrs. Arora had lit in Helena's house, where she was giving one of her parties. This was Lara's first meeting with the Aroras and she was suspicious of them, for she tended to associate all Indians with the manipulative holy men. And there was something manipulative about Mrs. Arora—literally, for she liked to fondle a person's hand, squeeze a shoulder, stroke a cheek. She had begun to do this to Lara, who jerked her head back and tossed her hair. Mrs. Arora smiled, and for the rest of the evening she treated her with a gentle deference that made it clear how she appreciated Lara as a special person. When someone admired a pearl brooch that Lara was wearing, Mrs. Arora stepped up closer to her—"May I?"—and delicately touched it. "How lovely," she murmured, leaving it ambiguous whether she meant Lara or her pearl.

Lara began to enjoy the party. The guests had an aura of cosmopolitan commerce that bordered on the artistic. They included several buyers from department stores—highly efficient businesswomen extensively traveled and with a trained eye for exotic products to bring home for sale; their own outfits reflected their cross-cultural good taste and each expertly appraised what the other was wearing. There was also a beauty queen from Bombay who was a model hoping to get into films, and one or two air hostesses hoping to get into modeling—all very decorative in cunning adaptations of Indian dress with jewelry and elaborate hairdos. They were modern and lively and very different from the Indians Lara had met in the holy places. She even began to tolerate the smell of the incense, which she realized was here used for aesthetic and no other effect and blended with the fragrance of the delicious dishes Mrs. Arora carried up from the kitchen. "Mummy, you're fantastic!" shrieked the Indian girls as they nibbled at kebabs held between their long, painted fingernails. Everyone liked Lara, and admired her clothes as they did one another's, and her pearl brooch—"It was my mother's," Angel heard her say. Soon she was calling Mrs. Arora "Mummy" like the other girls, and though she couldn't cook at all, asked for the recipe of her dum-dum potatoes.

Rohit was on duty at the airport and would be coming in later. Angel eagerly awaited him, anxious to have him meet Lara. Now was the moment for him to see her— Angel kept glancing at her across the room—when she was sparkling with enjoyment and no cloud between her and her own bright nature. Some of the girls had pushed back the chairs and were reclining on the carpet, and Lara appeared to be the center of that group. She also took up more space than anyone else, for while they sat with their legs crossed under them, she sprawled along the ground with her orange silk skirt spread around her. The front-door bell rang and Angel went running down—"Let him see her now," she thought—only it wasn't Rohit, it was Hugo come to drop in on the party. When he followed Angel into the room, there was a little stir among the girls; everyone had heard of Dr. Manarr, who wrote books and was famous. Lara's face darkened, but only for a moment; then she very slightly shifted her position so that her back was turned to him. By this time she had more to say than anyone, and her voice rose above theirs with little skips of enjoyment in it. Hugo lowered himself onto the sofa next to Helena so that they were in the place their parents had always been, while Anna and Siegfried hung just above them, still side by side on the flowered couch in the photograph taken by the German woman.

Hugo enjoyed looking at the group on the carpet. He always liked girls, and these were especially decorative. While Lara had her back to him, the others were by no means unaware of his presence; sometimes one of them would raise her eyes and meet his, only to look away again at once, adjust the garment over her bosom in a pretty gesture, and redouble her attention on Lara. "Oh, no, Lara, this is too much!" they protested, and she outshouted them: "But it's true, I swear!" She was recounting her Indian experiences and the exploits of the holy men she had met there.

"His women disciples were called Gopis—like Krishna's Gopis?—and on Fridays at the ritual bath each Gopi was allowed to wash a different part of him—"

"You're making it up!"

"I swear! And she carried the title for the whole week,

like one was the Gopi of the Left Arm, and another of the Right Arm, and the Gopi of the Navel, and of course the most honored position was—"

"Stop it!" They put their hands over their ears and one of them over Lara's mouth so that she sputtered the title exuberantly from behind it. And everyone else in the room enjoyed watching them have such a good time—themselves not unlike very fashionable Gopis in their bright Indian designer clothes, grouped around Lara, in her orange silk skirt, her face flushed with excitement. Angel kept thinking, "Why doesn't he come!" for this was the moment for Rohit to see her.

One of the girls—it was the beauty queen from Bombay—turned around to Hugo: "Oh, Dr. Manarr, can't you stop her telling us these awful fibs!"

"As if we believe a word of it!" called another, also addressing Hugo. "We know these people are bad but not that bad!" By this time all the girls had turned around to Hugo, and with so many beautiful eyes expectantly on him, he responded: "I could tell you about not dissimilar scenes in California—"

"Do tell!"

The doorbell rang and again Angel ran down and this time it was Rohit. He had come straight from the airport and was still in uniform; he said anxiously, "I'm not late?" At the foot of the stairs she leaned against him. He held her and whispered, "What's the matter?" but he could feel that it was pure joy that made her tremble. He kept his arm around her and they walked upstairs together and into the living room.

The scene had changed: the girls on the floor had

shifted toward Hugo and were looking up at him while he, lazily reclining with his legs stretched in front of him and his hands clasped behind his head, was entertaining them with anecdotes of California communes. And in the same way as they had done, listening to Lara, the girls laughed and protested they didn't believe a word of it. Lara was now somewhat isolated in the center of the room; her glow had faded, although her face was still flushed—her very fair skin suffused easily, with the blood flowing right up to her eyes. She wore a lot of mascara to outline and elongate these eyes, in which the gray-green irises swam around in a strange way.

When Angel led Rohit up to her she pulled him down to sit beside her on the floor. She made a great fuss over him—how much she had heard of him, how much Angel had talked about him so that she, Lara, was becoming quite jealous; she engrossed herself in him totally, oblivious of everyone else and especially of her father with his audience of pretty girls. Gratified by the charm her cousin lavished on her friend, Angel watched them together; yet she saw that Rohit did not respond as wholeheartedly as expected —as it was in his nature to do, for he was wide open to friendship. There was something stiff in the way he sat there; Angel thought it might be due to the jacket of his uniform, and she touched him on the shoulder, asking him to let her take it. He jumped up at once and stripped it off and hung it up himself; and afterward he went to help his mother carry around some syrupy candies she had made.

Meanwhile the girls around Hugo were getting more excited. He was telling them about a group specializing in animal natures, now roaring like lions, now trumpeting like elephants, to release the various bestial passions raging inside them. He waved his long arms and fingers around his head while mimicking the animal noises he described. Everyone watched, listened, and laughed; Hugo was no show-off but was glad to entertain the company. Only Angel noticed that Lara did not share in the general amusement. She lowered herself on the floor next to Lara and said, "It's just a joke."

"What a thing to joke about," said Lara. And suddenly she called across the room to him: "You're making yourself ridiculous!"

He stopped at once and said, "Yes, I've begun to suspect they're not laughing with but at."

"It's very embarrassing." Bitter scorn filled her voice. No one moved or spoke. The stage was Lara's—she had captured it and was now compelled to use it, whether she wanted to or not.

She said, "These are serious techniques, not party games." The words were reasonable but her tone had made Hugo alert. He sat up straight and drew in his legs; across the heads of the pretty girls at his feet, he looked only at his daughter as she continued: "They're used in theater training too—it's a famous method—there's a group in Poland who spend weeks in a forest somewhere—" Her voice broke with the strain of trying to control it.

"I know, I know," said Hugo with an uncharacteristic nervous edge.

"If you know, then why do you do it! Why do you upset me and ruin everything for me as usual!" She was anguished, and Angel wanted to put her arms around her as if to hold her back from some danger threatening her.

"What's wrong with you! He was being funny." This was Helena, sitting next to Hugo, an older, blowsier but also sturdier version of her niece. Hugo put his hand on her knee to silence her, but Helena went on more indignantly: "This is a *party,* everyone's supposed to be having fun."

"Daddy's idea of fun is to attack other people's beliefs and hurt their feelings. He did it to Mother and now he's doing it to me. No wonder she killed herself."

Probably only Angel right beside her heard this last sentence, because Mrs. Arora was crying out in distress: "I spent so many hours to make my gulab jamuns, and they have to be eaten *hot!*" She and Rohit circled the room with them. Rohit came over to Lara and bent down to offer her the dish. She shook her head, lowered pitifully to her breast. Rohit and Angel exchanged glances. He stood there in an attitude of suave service like an airline steward in first class, but his expression was one of compassion, so that Angel was confident that what she had hoped for would happen and he, too, would love her cousin.

Hugo took Lara home soon after; she linked her arm in his and allowed him to arrange her scarf around her throat against the weather. The rest of the guests also left, so that the party was over sooner than expected. Helena was annoyed, and she spoke critically of Lara, though Angel said several times, "She didn't mean it."

"She spoiled everyone's fun. I really don't like her."

"No, no," Angel said; she put her arm around her mother's neck in a conciliatory way.

"But I don't," Helena said.

"You will," Angel promised. "Everyone this evening did, didn't you think? I mean, at the beginning when she was in such wonderful spirits. And Rohit liked her afterward too."

"What about that pearl brooch she kept saying was her mother's?"

"Yes, it was mine, but she must have forgotten—it's such ages ago, anyone would forget."

It was the brooch that Lara had accepted from Angel when they were children. Its absence had first been noticed by their grandmother Anna, and when Angel confessed that she had given it away, both grandparents had been not dismayed but delighted by the child's generosity. Only Helena had been angry, with Angel for giving and Lara for taking.

SINCE ANGEL HAD grown up, her father no longer visited her at home but met her outside—usually for lunch in some very smart restaurant. For herself, she would have preferred a more modest place, especially after she became a vegetarian. Some obscure desire for physical purity had prompted her to this decision, for the sake she thought of her poetry. So when Peter took her to these sybaritic restaurants and lavishly ordered for himself, she ate a salad and drank water. "Are you sure that's all you want?" he asked dubiously, but fortunately did not allow his own enjoyment to be spoiled by her abstinence.

Angel brought Lara to meet Peter at one of these lunches, and this was a success. Lara liked the restaurant very much. It was crowded, packed with noisy people; the waiters shouted in Italian as they dashed from the kitchen with meats and soufflés freshly snatched from the ovens to be delivered in prime condition to the tables. People sat close together on green sofas all along the walls, the service tables were heaped with fruits, cheeses, and crystal bowls of elaborate desserts, wall-size mirrors redoubled the crowded scene and the Venetian lusters illumining it. Lara felt at home there, and also with Peter. They had a favored place in a corner sofa, and the maître d' whispered to him what to order today; Peter didn't have to see the list to know which wine to select. Lara joined him wholeheartedly in everything, and they even tasted from each other's plates. "You don't know what you're missing," Peter told the abstemious Angel; and Lara said, "Oh, she's just this little saint," passing her hand over Angel's short crop of curls. Peter said, "I wonder where she got it from;" he leaned back to laugh, extending his stomach inside his vest and making it obvious that it wasn't from him.

At this time of day most of the patrons were businessmen, some of them accompanied by girlfriends who were models or actresses, professionally pretty and perfectly groomed. But Lara stood out, and many men looked at her, directly at the table or in the mirror, and this made her check repeatedly on her reflection. She was as usual in very bright colors and hung about with jewelry; her general gypsy air was heightened by her vibrant manner and the dark makeup around her eyes. She was flushed with wine and excitement at the admiration she aroused in the other guests, and the waiters, in Peter, and in herself at what she saw in the mirror. And as she glowed, so did Angel with pride in her. Peter was enjoying himself, he listened and poured wine for her with a smile on his full, moist lips. She had so much to tell, and when in the mood, as now, told it so well, with gestures and mimicry, about her dancing, her acting, her schools, her travels in far-off places: her life as exotic as her appearance. People leaving the restaurant passed closer by their table than necessary, the waiters came up often, and Peter lit a cigar with his coffee. The maître d'hôtel sent liqueurs on the house—also one for Angel, which Lara drank after she had finished her own, her cheeks burning.

The tables were almost all empty and some of the waiters had sat down at the back to eat their own meal. Angel was uncomfortable, aware that everyone was waiting for them to leave, but Lara did not let up in animation. Absent-mindedly opening packets of sugar, she scattered it over the tablecloth (Angel tried to brush it into a heap and get rid of it in a saucer). Lara looked around for more coffee but Peter had finished with his cigar, so he glanced toward the waiter, who stood ready with the check. Peter stood up with his accustomed gesture of patting both breast pockets to make sure he hadn't forgotten anything. Lara continued sitting, for she didn't realize or couldn't believe that it was over— she looked up at Peter and blinked a bit in bewilderment as though she had just emerged from a different mode of existence, like a dream or a spellbinding performance given by herself.

Coming out of the restaurant into the street was rather like leaving a theater, with a sense of letdown after heightened sensations. Peter, already wearing a preoccupied business face, thanked the girls for their company but made it clear that he was off in an opposite direction. Lara said, "When am I going to see you again?" She could and did say this quite frankly, for wasn't she a niece to him? And laying her hand on his arm, she added, "Uncle Peter," smiling up at him in a way that didn't make him feel like an uncle. He looked down at her, their eyes met, her hand was still on his arm; and she left it there till he said, "Yes, we must do it again soon." Then they both remembered Angel, who stood waiting for them.

Peter remembered something else—something difficult, so that his face changed: "Have you been to see your grandmother? She's fired her maid again."

"Oh, no," Angel said.

"Oh, yes," said Peter. Grandmother Koenig's old maid, Lina, had died about a year earlier, and ever since she had had a succession of maids, none of them lasting out a week.

"I'll go now," Angel promised. Peter nodded and parted from them. Lara, still in a wonderful mood, tucked her arm under Angel's, and together they moved through the crowded streets. Lara walked fast and with a skip every few steps; a current of energy flowed from her through Angel's arm. The weather had turned very warm, many people had taken off their coats and looked uncharacteristically carefree. In the sunlight, brand-new structures reflected each other in sides made entirely of glass; fountains played in their atriums and trees waved on their lofty summits, where roof gardens met the sky with white clouds and silver airplanes floating in it.

When they reached Grandmother Koenig's apartment building, Lara was not yet ready to part from Angel. Still holding her arm tightly pressed, she came into the lobby with her. Here among the marble walls and pillars stood Empire sofas in dark velvet, little shaded lamps, and gilt tubs full of flowers that looked artificial even though they were not. The very old doormen knew Angel but nevertheless had to announce her, and while they waited for Grandmother Koenig to answer, Lara whispered, "Shall I come with you? . . . Let me, I want to." Angel did not refuse her—she could not—though doubtful of her grandmother's mood. She would have liked to warn Lara, but they were trapped with an ancient employee who took them up in his highly polished mahogany elevator.

Grandmother Koenig stood waiting for them in her doorway—she carried a feather duster and was in a militant mood. She didn't even ask who Lara was but launched straight into the saga of the latest maid whom she had caught applying brass polish on the silver. "These are the sort of people they send you nowadays," said Grandmother Koenig, and she laughed for the pity of it. "But don't worry, I can do the work myself a hundred times better than any of these poor creatures the agency sends me to ruin my good things." And to prove her competence, she flicked the feather duster over the nearest piece of furniture. She had put on a little apron over her crepe dress, but this in no way detracted from her majesty.

When she had flicked enough, she allowed Angel to relieve her of the duster and to coax her to sit down with them. Now Lara could be introduced to her—"Your cousin? Hugo's daughter? Helena's niece?" But although she caught on to the family relationship at once, she was not gracious. In fact, she said bluntly that it was not a good time for her to receive visitors because, as they could see for themselves, she was alone and could not serve anything— "Grandma, we don't want anything! We just had lunch with Peter—"

"Peter? Why didn't he come with you? He knows I'm

alone. I don't expect his wife and children to come visit me
—I know they're much too busy, and why should they, I'm
only his old mother and now I don't even have a maid to
serve coffee." She snorted through her nose—with indignation; she didn't feel sorry for herself: on the contrary, she
appeared proud of her own immaculate appearance and that
of her apartment, which in spite of unsatisfactory service
was polished and waxed to perfection, with dried flowers
arranged in the waist-high vases.

"If you had telephoned, I could have gone down to
Greenberg's to buy cakes for you—they're not bad, though
nothing like what Marie used to make. Marie could make
anything—strudel, Sacher, all the things your grandfather
loved till the doctors wouldn't let him eat them anymore.
But you don't remember Marie, you only knew Lina, who
was by training a parlor maid and not a cook at all but at
least she tried, poor soul, which is more than you can say of
any of these people who come today and call themselves
domestic servants." She drummed her fingers on the arms
of her chair, impatient with the subject and herself for
dwelling on it. For the first time she turned her attention to
Lara: "You're like your aunt," she said abruptly.

It was dark in the room, for the light from the chandeliers was largely absorbed by the curtains and upholstery.
Ever since they had come in, Lara had sat uncharacteristically still in one of the brown armchairs. Her radiance appeared to be eclipsed, so Angel was surprised when Grandmother Koenig nevertheless recognized the likeness to
Helena. Eager to hear more, Angel said, "Mother must
have been just Lara's age when you first saw her."

"The first time Peter brought her, she was wearing a

skirt that color." She pointed at Lara's bright dress. "And a shawl. Afterward I told Peter, why don't you take her to Bergdorf's and buy her something she can meet people in. I even said, let her use my charge card. I'm not suggesting her family couldn't afford to buy her whatever was necessary, but we thought it would be a gracious way of telling her what was expected in our family. Of course, she never went, and that was just the beginning." Grandmother Koenig's mouth turned down in its usual way at the mention of her son's first marriage; and went down even farther as she continued on his second: "At least one thing I can say about your mother, she didn't come in here looking around to see what she could expect to get when I'm gone. Not like the other one with her little eyes going this way and that—"

"Is that Peter's wife?" Lara asked, stirring for the first time since she had vanished into the armchair. But although Angel had been waiting for this moment to show Lara off, now she quickly intervened, "Oh, never mind, don't let's upset Grandma."

"Upset me!" laughed Grandmother Koenig. "And why should I be upset? It's my poor son who is married to her and has to hear her shrill little voice day and night and that accent she never did get rid of though she thinks she has. I don't even need to see her, and heaven knows I see little enough of her except when she comes to check up on the silver she is hoping for. Don't think I've forgotten what happened when Lina passed away," she warned. She turned to Lara: "Lina expired here in this room."

"Oh, Grandma, Lara doesn't have to hear about it," Angel pleaded.

"Here on this carpet," continued Grandmother Koenig, pointing at the very spot, not far from where Lara was sitting. "Well, all right, Lina was old, she was very cranky, she was deaf, she didn't bathe often enough, she couldn't cook, but my goodness, she was a human being and she had been with me for over forty years. That counts for something. I found her."

"Here?" said Lara, looking at the spot.

"Here on this carpet. I wasn't at all well myself that day, so I had gone to Dr. Herzberg who told me, 'Mrs. Koenig, it's pure stress; nervous stress.' When I came home I called for Lina to go to the pharmacy for the new prescription. She didn't answer, but that didn't surprise me, for she was very deaf and never so deaf as when I wanted her for something. And then I came in here and I saw her. She had fallen on her face on the carpet with her arms spread out and she was still holding her feather duster. So you could say she died in harness, which is the best way. I was sorry, of course, for her, and also I knew it was not going to be easy to find a new person, which is exactly what has happened. My mind wasn't clear that day—I had been to the doctor, he emphatically said I was suffering from nervous stress and now I come home and find my maid on my carpet. Naturally, I was confused, I didn't know what to do. I have to admit I definitely didn't like to be in the same room with her, so I stood outside the door and looked in at her and then I phoned Peter. *She* answered, and when I told her what had happened—"

"Grandma, Lara doesn't even *know* Lilian!"

Calm and stately, intent only on giving an impartial account of the facts, Grandmother Koenig turned to Lara:

"She said that she and Peter were giving a dinner party for someone very important from the bank, that the guests would be arriving within the hour, that under no circumstances could she or Peter leave the house and that she wasn't even going to tell Peter, who was upstairs relaxing in his herbal bath—"

"But that's terrible!" cried Lara. "That's really awful! She must be a dreadful person!" She had leaped up.

Grandmother Koenig, pleased with this positive response, continued: "That's only one story, and there are many others I could tell. And *you* could tell," she said to Angel.

"Why, what did she do to you?" Lara blazed up more.

Grandmother Koenig looked at her in approval, forgiving her too-bright, too-bohemian clothes: "You're a good height—of course your father is tall, and your aunt, and your grandparents, the whole Manarr family. I don't know what happened with this child." She pointed at Angel. "Perhaps it was all those illnesses you had—always some fever, or earache, and throwing up your food—that's what must have stunted your growth." She sighed for Angel, and wanted to do something nice for her. "Come and kiss your grandmother Koenig. You remember how happy you were with me when you used to come for lunch, just you and I chatting away, and Lina cooked for us. Well, those were the good times, they won't come again."

LARA CAUGHT HOLD of the idea that Angel had been mistreated as a child by Peter's second family. She felt it to be a bond between herself and her cousin. When it came to unhappy childhoods, Lara was a front contender, so Angel felt almost guilty for the blissful years she had spent with her mother and grandparents. As for Peter's second family—Lilian and her three boys—they had certainly done their best for Angel whenever she was sent to them. But it was the same as at Grandmother Koenig's—she had missed her mother so unbearably that she had spent all her time with them in tears. They lived on the Hudson within reach of the city, in a large house ideal for the games Peter's boys so vigorously played. They were several years younger than Angel but did their best to take care of her. All their efforts were in vain: what Angel remembered principally about those visits was sitting sobbing by the swimming pool, surrounded by the three little boys trying to comfort her. They were skinny and sunburned in their swimsuits, and Angel looked large, awkward, and very white beside them. When her sobs grew uncontrollable, they called their mother; and however busy she was—and Lilian was always busy, she was building up an extensive social life—she, too, did her best to solace Angel. It was not until she asked her whether she wanted to be taken home that Angel raised her head and dried her tears. So then Lilian had to get her car out and the boys crowded around to say good-bye. Angel's heart grew lighter and lighter the nearer they got to home, while Lilian in the driver's seat beside her sat biting her lip, wondering how to explain having to bring her stepchild home again.

Angel reflected ruefully that she had not really improved much since those days. She still did not want to be anywhere except at home or venture far beyond the streets around her house. These she loved as passionately as others love nature; they were the ambience of her imagination, the bones and body of her thought. And when it was a question of figuring a world beyond and other than this world of streets and traffic, there was for her no correlative more poignant than the first lights coming on in the windows and pricking into the texture of dusk visible between the new apartment buildings; or the commercial signs floating pale and watery on the night sky till they faded away at dawn in deference to an even more delicate shade of light.

The wild longing she had had as a child for her mother now lay quiescent; but Helena was still the center of the home Angel lived in and loved. Although there were just the two of them in the house, they had no thoughts of selling it. Besides turning the basement into an office, they also used some of the upstairs rooms to store the merchandise they imported; but that in no way encroached on the intimate character of the house, which was retained in the furniture, the flowered upholstery, pastel carpets, and Tiffany lamps belonging to Anna and Siegfried: and, of course, for each of them, for Helena and Angel, in the presence of the other. This did not prevent Helena from getting annoyed with Angel for staying cooped in at home too much. She would come up the stairs to Angel's bedroom and find her sitting in the dark. When she turned on the light, Angel cried out, for not only did it pierce her eyes but also her mind, dwelling in some dark and quiet place.

"Is this how you are going to spend your whole life?" Helena once asked her. "No wonder your father is always on about how I'm making you waste your time. *I'm* making you! He should see you sitting here, staring out the window or God knows what it is you're doing. . . . What *are* you doing?"

"No, nothing," Angel said, which was the literal truth. "When did you see Peter?"

"You will not believe this: I ran into him on the street." She flung the large hat she wore on Angel's bed. Her gray-streaked hair, which she now wore twisted around at the back of her head, had come loose, and she peered to fix it in Angel's small round wall mirror. "Peter is getting jowly, and his color was very high, but I guess that was from the martinis he had with his wonderful two-hour five-course lunch. . . . What do you think, Angel, have I lost weight? No need to be nice, it's more helpful to tell the truth. But I think you're right—definitely right—because last month this dress felt quite tight around here, and now it's all right, almost. Peter asked me about Lara—he said you'd brought her to lunch with him? Why?"

"Well, I don't know," Angel said. "Why not."

"That's a typical Angel sort of answer. People usually know why they do something—other people, that is. Anyway, he liked her."

Angel brightened: "What did he say?"

"He thought it was good for you to have a friend your own age and someone so lively who'd bring you out more. Bring you out where, he didn't say, but I suppose he meant out from here, from me—no, he's right! We're together far too much."

"Do you really believe that?" Angel said to this last statement and mostly to the sad note in it.

"Your father does. He also seems to think that you and

Lara get along very well together. That you like her very much." When no answer came—"Well, do you?"

"Yes," Angel said. She reflected, for it was her habit to try to find accurate words to convey her meaning. "Yes, I do. I love her."

"How you talk." Helena pulled pins out of her hair to have the satisfaction of jabbing them back again. "You don't know her all that well, or all that long. You don't really know her at all, and I must tell you—not that I'm trying to set you against her—but she *is* difficult. Hugo is having a very difficult time with her at home." She clamped her lips together, not that she wouldn't have liked to say more, but in face of Angel's silence. When this had gone on too long: "I'm only telling you what Hugo said. And he is her father, and a psychiatrist." She could see that Angel was working around in her mind to find the right words—perhaps to dispute the finality of both these qualifications—so quickly gathering up her hat, and bag stuffed with business papers, she said, "I have no idea why we spend so much time talking about Lara."

LARA ATTENDED ACTING classes in a studio downtown. The teacher was a famous drama coach of thirty years ago who was now very old and fierce so that her students were terrified of her, except her few favorites, of whom Lara was one. Lara said that she had very wise and wonderful eyes, and a way of teaching that was by intuition rather than direct tuition. Lara was very eager to please her, and every day she brought her a fresh rose to pin to her blouse. She also worked hard at home on the texts she was given to present in class. She made Angel read with her, which was very satisfactory for Angel but less so for Lara because, as she said once or twice, taking the book away from Angel, she might as well emote against a piece of wood. But however much she enjoyed these sessions, Angel could not bring herself to put more expression—or indeed any expression—into the part she had to read. While Lara reveled in throwing herself into another character, Angel mumbled and scuffed her feet; yet she never refused, she gamely took the book and stood there with it—solid, four-square—while Lara took wing.

Angel didn't know in advance when she would be called upon to render this service. Lara either showed up at the house or called Angel to meet her somewhere. Angel waited for her, and even after several days with no sign from Lara, she kept on waiting. When Rohit, who came almost daily on business from his mother, asked her to accompany him for a walk or a movie, she said she couldn't because she had a date with her cousin. Yet in the past she and Rohit had been each other's constant companions. When she refused, Rohit never showed disappointment, he just said, "Tomorrow, then." And she would agree yes, tomorrow, though she knew this didn't depend on herself. However many times she broke her promise, Rohit always accepted its renewal for the next day as perfectly valid. Once, when he had already run down the stairs, she called after him, "No, wait! I'll come!" He was pleased, he stood and waited for her. When they got in the street, he took her hand and swung it to and fro, and she, too, was happy that they were together. But then a telephone rang—"Is that ours?"—and she had to hurry back, quickly open the door with her key, out of breath when she answered. It wasn't Lara, but then Angel thought that next time it might be, so she had better not leave.

There were a frenzied few weeks when Lara worked very hard for a performance the students were giving before

an invited audience. But this didn't come to anything—
perhaps the performance was canceled—and Lara no longer
needed Angel's assistance so frequently nor, when they
met, did she talk of the classes with the same enthusiasm.
There followed a whole week when Angel didn't see or
hear from her, and when she went to Hugo's apartment to
find her, she wasn't there. Hugo's secretary said that he was
with a patient but would be free soon, so Angel decided to
wait.

When he first moved into this apartment, Hugo had
hired a designer, who had furnished it with ultramodern
pieces and in bland colors blending so harmoniously into
the space that they were practically invisible and certainly
unnoticeable. There was an extensive view of the park from
all the lofty windows, but this, too, seemed impersonal—a
real estate agent's display of trees and water ringed around
by the jagged edge of architectural skyline. The only intimate note inside the rooms came from the assorted rugs and
antique lamps Hugo had picked up in company with various girlfriends who loved to spend Saturday mornings at
the auction houses.

As soon as his patient left, Hugo called Angel into his
study. Here everything was meaningful—the pattern of the
Afghan carpet, the primitive tribal objects, the modern ab-
stracts, and the framed mandalas drawn by yogis or psychot-
ics. Hugo looked exhausted, and Angel guessed that this
was from his work with his patient. She felt sorry for him
and thought how intolerable it must be to receive the bur-
den of someone else's inner life on top of one's own. However, soon he was smiling at her in his wan way and thanked

her for coming to see her dull old uncle. She said truthfully that she was always glad to be with him, and even more truthfully that she had actually come to see Lara. He sat up in surprise: "But don't you know? She's moved out . . . I thought *you'd* know."

"I haven't seen her for a week."

"It's a week since she left. No, she didn't tell me where she went, she didn't want me to have a phone number, though no doubt Peter can tell you." At her look of surprise: "Peter Koenig. Your father," he added with an unamused laugh.

Angel did not feel composed, but looked it, with her hands remaining folded in her lap. She said, "Does Mother know?"

"Not from me. I thought maybe it'll all disappear and she'll be back today, tomorrow. But it's a week now. I called that studio place she's been going to, but all they could tell me was that her fees were due. I sent them a check, though I'm not sure she'll be going there again." He laid his fingertips on his closed eyelids for a moment before continuing: "Something happened at the studio. Something to do with a show they were putting on—do you know about it? Lara was to be in it and then she wasn't . . . Angel, what shall I tell you? Well, I might as well." He sighed but seemed relieved that someone was there to hear.

On Sunday morning he had had a friend with him— her husband, another psychiatrist, was away on a weekend conference, so she had stayed the night. It had happened before, with this friend and others; in fact, it happened most weekends—"Angel, who likes to be alone on the weekend?" Sometimes Lara was friendly and joined them for breakfast. But that morning she had stayed in her room. Hugo had felt waves of personality coming from behind her door, and this made him hurry his companion, who was cozily chatting while eating her grapefruit. But he was grateful to her, for she had been very nice to him, so while he was helping her on with her coat in the hall, he kissed her. Lara chose that moment to appear—there was no need for her to come that way at all; if his friend's presence offended her, she could easily have left her room without encountering them. But she stood there, barefoot, a robe thrown over her nightdress, supporting herself with one arm on the door frame: all those waves he had felt emanating from her now concentrated in her hostile presence. His friend drew away from him, patted his cheek in good-bye, said something pleasant to Lara, and left. Hugo also tried to say something pleasant—he offered Lara coffee, said it was still hot—but she turned from him and walked away, solidly planting her bare feet, the belt of her robe trailing behind her.

He had gone to his study to work on his book. Yes, he was writing another book—here he digressed to talk about it. He admitted that although both a doctor and a psychiatrist, he was no longer interested in sick people. His work was with the healthy, his aim to make them super-healthy by putting them in touch with fields of energy that lay ready to be tapped within their own psyche. The theory was simple, the technique incredibly difficult—"You know that yourself, Angel, from writing poetry."

"I don't write poetry," Angel said. "Not really," she qualified. "Not yet. What about Lara?"

After a while Lara had followed him into his study, disturbing his work. She had always been completely indifferent to his work. She said she had no support from him, not in anything. He cared nothing for her career as an actress—here he said eagerly that of course he cared and wasn't he coming to the performance on, when was it? The sixth? "That's canceled," she said abruptly. "Not canceled, but I'm not in it. You see, that's how much you care, you have no idea what's happening in my life. But don't worry about me! I'm doing just fine without you, professionally—*and* personally, if you must know," she ended up, changing the subject and her mood: she looked at him sideways, quite mischievously as with a secret she might or might not share with him.

Hugo told Angel, "When I see her like that, at certain angles, with certain expressions, I see her mother."

"But she's like *my* mother!"

"Of course she is, I'm not saying she's not, but there *is* Alice in her, and Alice's family, she does have that strain, Angel, and Peter will have to be very careful."

For this was the secret Lara had not taken long to let him in on: she was having an affair with Peter Koenig. Hugo admitted to Angel that he had laughed—he couldn't help it, it had been his immediate reaction. Realizing at once how wrong it was, he had composed his features, but it was too late. She told him that she turned to Peter for everything he himself, her own father, had failed her in. Peter had strength and stability, and that was what she lacked in her life, and what her mother had lacked—she always had her mother as a last unanswerable argument against Hugo. He sat silent and with his head lowered as though he felt guilty—which he didn't at all and there was plenty he could have said to a more impartial witness about his marriage; and about Peter's too.

Then she told him she was moving out. She presented this decision as one she had come to after mature deliberation, whereas he was sure she had thought of it only that moment. And having made it, she couldn't wait to put it into action. She went out of the room and he heard her immediately after on the telephone. Presumably she was making arrangements, but they did not appear to be conclusive, for this first call was followed by several more during the course of the day. In between she banged around her room, packing up. The calls continued—when the phone rang, she snatched it up and talked into it in a low and occasionally tearful voice. To Hugo she was now charming, and she suggested a quiet supper at home for the two of them. He canceled a date he had for that evening, and Lara made scrambled eggs for them—tried to anyway, but they stuck to the pan and he came to her rescue, though he couldn't cook any better than she could, which made her tease him that the two of them really were not meant to set up housekeeping together. She stayed in a sweet mood all evening and next day she left.

USUALLY, WHEN ANGEL and her father met, they arrived at the same time, for both were very punctual; but

that day—the day after she learned of Lara's disappearance
—he was late and she watched him hurry across the cocktail lounge of the hotel that was their meeting place. Strip-
ping off his Burberry to hand over to the hat-check girl, he
turned to look for Angel with his characteristic gesture of
patting both sides of his double-breasted suit. He saw her at
once, for he had the keen glance of a captain of industry;
and it was with such a captain's authority that he made his
way toward her across the crowded room. The adjectives
strong, solid, reliable, which Lara had applied to him, sat
comfortably on his shoulders—especially in contrast with
the other people there enjoying their cocktail hour: a des-
perately thin woman with red hair and a young man who
may have been a son, or at least took the place of one; an
impassive bald bejeweled middle-aged man with a handsome youth; some very smart girls perched on stools at the
bar, pretending to be engrossed in conversation with each
other—none of them looked as though they were at the
end of a day's work. Only Peter, managing to stride though
having to maneuver his way through an entanglement of
little tables, appeared to have just come from his counting-
house.

He could not begin to defend himself soon enough,
and when Angel said nothing, he said more and more. He
told her that after their lunch together Lara had called him
at home that same evening. Next day she had called again
in the office, and on the third day he had agreed to meet
her for a drink. It had been in this same hotel—he pointed
at the table where they had sat—and Angel looked and saw
another couple there. It was one of the girls who had been
sitting at the bar and now was making animated conversa-

tion to a young man who let her put herself out for him. Just so Lara must have put herself out for Peter, often touching his sleeve as she talked; Angel knew how vivacious and charming Lara could be.

Peter said that she had told him about her damaged childhood, her difficult relationship with her father, about her mother; she told him everything and he could see that she was an unhappy human being who needed help; and, moreover, a sort of niece. "What could I do?" Peter said. "I couldn't tell her leave me alone, go home." Yet Angel knew that if Lara hadn't been as she was, he could have told her so very easily—probably had quite a lot of experience at it and could be as cool as the young man across the room who was at that moment flicking a speck of dust from the sleeve the girl so intimately touched.

Peter said that they had spent an afternoon in a motel just outside the city; then a few more afternoons and finally a couple of nights there, which had involved him in some complicated lies to his wife. With this last admission Peter grew even more florid than usual and had to whip out his handkerchief to wipe his face. He spoke of the telephone calls on Sunday morning, and again he appealed to Angel: "How could I tell her leave me alone?" They had telephoned to and fro—he had had to sneak out of the house, drive to the station, and wait for a man to conclude a deal on the pay phone. As the day wore on, he had become the more desperate of the two—Lara had known exactly what she wanted and had feared no complications. But for him there had been the fear of complication with his wife; and also of Lara, that she might turn elsewhere if he failed her.

"Yes," said Angel, "she could have called me."

Her father played with some book matches on the ash-tray; he lit one and didn't blow it out till it almost burned his fingers. He mumbled that he wouldn't want to lose her. When he realized that "her" might be construed as ambig-uous, he said he meant Angel.

She said, "Why should you lose me?"

"No, of course not . . . Not you—nor her." He gave her a swift glance, half embarrassed, half pleading.

She did not absolve him; her mild gaze did not beam on him with her usual affection. She blamed him, although no one knew better than she did how difficult it was to deny Lara anything she momentarily desired.

LARA CALLED ANGEL that same evening. She had gone to live in the motel where she and Peter had spent some afternoons, but she said she wanted to move out and back to the city. She went into no preliminaries or explana-tions, rightly assuming that Angel knew the facts. She asked her to come and fetch her: "Dying to see you," she said; she made kissing noises and hung up.

Angel pondered how to get there. She wanted to keep Helena in ignorance for as long as possible; and it might be possible forever, since Lara was returning to the city. Angel decided to hire a car, and since she couldn't drive, she would have to take Rohit with her and so let him into the secret.

She went at once to the Aroras' apartment; but that evening everything there was strange to her and unfamiliar, including Rohit. He opened the door to her in Indian dress, white muslin kurta and pajama, and with saffron-colored smears on his forehead. Sounds of chanted prayer came from behind the closed door of the bedroom. There was always a savor of incense lingering in the apartment, but now it was thick and smoldering and mixed in with the smell of garlands of marigolds which were beginning to wilt. Indian dress made Rohit look remote—in place, time, civilization—and this impression was enhanced by the sounds of the mysterious rite and the marks of it on his forehead.

He explained that a brahmin living in Queens had come to conduct a ceremony for a death anniversary. He hesitated for a moment before saying that it was for his brother. Angel had always assumed Rohit to be an only child—hence the passionate attachment between him and his mother—but now he said that he had had an elder brother who had died four years ago on this day, aged twenty-five. Angel felt that she could not speak of her request now, but Rohit, realizing that she had come on a special errand, urged her to tell him. She only mentioned about driving the car, and he agreed at once, promising to take the day off tomorrow.

The door of the bedroom opened, and Mrs. Arora came gliding out. She was draped in a pure white sari and had laid aside all her jewelry; only her eyes shone, with tears, and her hair was its usual brilliant black. The brahmin went on with his sacred chant, but then stuck his head out the door to see what was going on. He scrutinized Angel, and after Mrs. Arora had explained her in Hindi, returned inside and, revving himself up with some hawking and spitting, continued to chant. Mrs. Arora kissed Angel's forehead and touched her with loving gestures, but she said nothing and did not refer to the ceremony or whom it was for.

NEXT DAY IN the car Angel found it difficult to tell Rohit what had happened, for there were no extenuating circumstances she could offer for her father and Lara. She knew that Rohit had a simple, straightforward morality not unlike her own, although she herself had no difficulty accepting the situation because of so totally accepting the two people involved. After she had told him, Rohit said nothing and drove staring ahead. But when she stole a glance at him, she saw that it was not disapproval but yesterday's sadness that lingered in his face. He did not again speak of his brother, and she could not ask.

The motel flashed VACANCIES in multicolored neon, and there were so many that Lara seemed to be the only occupant. However, she said that there were always guests for an hour or two in the afternoons, and it got really busy in the evening, when people drove out from the city, including Peter (she mentioned him easily, in passing). It did not seem like a pleasure spot—a row of prefabricated units on a vacant plot of land just off the highway, next to an abandoned gas station. One of the units served as an office, and here refreshments could be had from a machine. A fat woman sat in the office, the proprietress, with whom Lara was on very friendly terms and introduced as Wendy. She said that Wendy made coffee in the mornings and served it in plastic cups with frozen Danish heated up. "Delicious," said Lara, making a horrid face behind Wendy's back.

Angel had hoped that she would be taking Lara home

with her, but instead they drove to a hotel in the city, overlooking the park, where a suite had been reserved. It was a far cry from the motel—a luxury suite with fine carpets, some pieces of period furniture, and fruit and flowers by courtesy of the management. From between looped curtains the windows framed a view of trees and horse-drawn carriages with liveried coachmen. Lara was delighted: she wandered around the suite, found the room service menu, and at once suggested a party, with champagne in an ice bucket. When Rohit said he had to go—to return the rented car and to be with his mother—she was devastated, evidently treasuring his company, though she had never before shown much interest in him. She pleaded and wheedled till he agreed to stay for a while, and then she brightened at once and completely overrode Angel, who tried to make him leave to be with his mother.

She really was in a great party mood and did not seem to notice the lack of it in her guests. This may have been because both of them were by nature withdrawn—spectators rather than actors, whereas she, of course, was born to take the stage, in life if not in art. She spoke of that subject, of her career as a performer, though she was no longer sure what form her performance might take. Her acting had been completely spoiled for her by the teacher at the studio. It might have been all right if she had known her thirty years before, but now she was old: "Old old old—and vain, you would not believe!" How was it possible to respect a person so vain and in love with herself? "This is how she arrives in class," said Lara, and she jumped up to demonstrate the primping walk, fingers daintily splayed, of an old fat, corseted woman teetering on heels too high and in youthful slacks too tight over her elephantine hindquarters. Of course the really ambitious students knew how to flatter her—and there was always one who had a flower for her, her favorite red rose. Here Lara mimicked how she received this gift with a start of glad surprise and pursed her mouth as she tucked it into the far-too-deep opening of her blouse. Lara said it used to make her feel sick to see an old person make a spectacle of herself and young people playing up to her.

Lara spoke of music as a possible choice for herself. She said she had always been passionate about it, and although not very musical, she had tried at various times to learn various instruments. The one she had enjoyed the most was the flute. She had had an ordinary little reed flute with which she had gone out to sit by herself in a meadow by a stream, and she had played: she showed how, curled up in an armchair in the hotel suite with her yellow skirt spread around her. She said she had known a woman who could play from her throat—the sweetest warbling sounds, you could never have believed it was not a flute. Lara tapped the side of her neck and tried to mimic the sounds and couldn't, so she sang them instead and laughed; only her laughter sounded beautiful.

Angel did not enjoy the performance as much as she usually enjoyed everything that Lara did. It probably had to do with Rohit. He had not yet recovered from yesterday's mood, but it was not only that: there was something in the way he looked at Lara, grave and reserved, as though he were reserving his own thoughts about her. It made Angel uneasy, and if she had been less fond of him, she would have blamed him for marring her own pleasure in her cousin's company.

ANGEL WAS SITTING in the basement office, typing up orders, when Helena burst in: "Is your father mad? Is he completely out of his mind?" So she had found out.

Angel finished typing a line, mainly to get her wits together.

"And you *knew.* Hugo says you've known for *days.*" Helena seized Angel's shoulder and shook it. "Did you think it was no business of mine? Not that it is—why should I care what my niece does with my ex-husband— but that you should keep quiet, keep it a secret from me—" And again she shook Angel's shoulder and squeezed it hard till Angel said she was hurting her.

Helena sank down onto an office chair that looked as if it might collapse under her great weight. She was breathing too heavily to speak for a while, and when she did, it was in a different tone: "Since when have we had secrets from each other?"

Angel got down on the floor by her mother's chair and took her hand. She laid it against her cheek. "I thought it would blow over and that you would never need to know. . . . Not never but not till later, when it wouldn't mean anything anymore."

"Does it now?"

Angel couldn't answer because she didn't know. She really had no experience of affairs of this nature, and she was aware that something that appeared momentous to her might not to anyone else, not even the main protagonists. Helena knew this and went on to say, *"You're* the one that's most stirred up and that's what's made you change. Yes, you have! . . . You've even stopped writing poetry."

"I never started."

"Oh, that's not true. No, let go my hand. You're not being my own Angel now."

"I just used to make up these little poems as a child— it's not as if I ever seriously did it—"

"Then what do you seriously do?" said Helena.

"You know I keep busy." Angel waved her hand around the office. "There's a lot—"

"If I thought that's all you did—all right, even if you weren't actually writing poetry, I'm sure you did more than just sit here, thinking about those stupid accounts, or about Lara."

Angel made no attempt to defend herself. When Helena spoke again, she sounded not angry but truly puzzled: "You've never been like this before, with anyone. Don't I know it? Wasn't I waiting for you"—she ran her hand over Angel's crop of wiry curls—"to go on dates or bring someone home or have those phone calls other girls have . . . I'm not complaining. I knew you didn't need anyone because you were happy to be at home, to be with me. I kept thinking, well later, she's not ready yet, there'll be someone. And anyway, she's much too good for anyone. Of course you are, darling, yes, yes, you are. Kiss me. And again. Kiss me again." When Angel had finished kissing her, Helena was smiling: "That's what we said from the day you were born, your grandparents and I—there'll never be anyone good enough for our Angel. And it was always our idea that you'd stay home in your little room up there, writing poetry, doing what we ourselves wanted to but couldn't—like Papa with his singing lessons and me with my boutiques. It's like people who don't pray themselves are glad someone else is doing it, nuns and so on. You were our own little nun—you always did look a bit like one, you still do, except I wish you would occasionally wear something other than that skirt that I should have thrown out long ago."

Angel looked down at herself; she smiled and shrugged. Then she said: "But Lara's like you. Don't you think she looks fabulous? Whatever she wears, it's beautiful. Just like you. That's why I admire her so," she said ingenuously. She added, even more ingenuously: "I guess that's why Peter admires her too."

"Oh, Peter. Peter Koenig. As though he'd wait to jump into bed with anyone because they remind him of *me.*" She hesitated on the brink of saying more on the same subject, but changed her mind. Instead, she said, "I hope he knows she's highly neurotic. I hope you know."

Angel drew away from her mother. She got up from the floor and went back to her desk.

"We have to face facts," Helena pursued her.

"It's not a fact."

"Hugo says it is." Helena couldn't meet her daughter's gaze, mild as moonlight though it was. But she persisted: "He's told me himself that she's sick."

"And if she is—then shouldn't we be looking after her? Taking care of her?"

"Oh, is that what you're doing!" said Helena. She got up from her chair, knocking it over. "Taking care of a sick person; a patient. You and Peter Koenig—two sisters of mercy. Oh, don't say any more, I don't want to hear any more! No, no, go, leave me alone." She turned her face away—just as she used to when Angel was a child and she was very angry with her. At that time Angel used to feel that there was no earth under her feet or sky above her head so that she might as well be in hell or some such pit of desolation. But now this was not so; she seemed to have grown roots of strength she didn't even know about. Of course she was still sorry for any discord between herself and her mother, but now it was for Helena's sake, who appeared to suffer from it more than she did.

PETER TELEPHONED ANGEL—but not to talk about Lara; he said, "Mother fell and broke her arm." He gave her some more details and hung up, saying "Thanks," for he knew that she would at once go and see her grandmother.

A new maid opened the door and showed Angel into the drawing room, where Grandmother Koenig sat enthroned in her chair. Except that her arm was in plaster and in a sling, she looked the same as usual, and also as usual began at once to speak of the shortcomings of the maid. Angel interrupted her to ask about the accident, but all that Grandmother Koenig would tell her was that it had been due to the carelessness of the previous maid who, after vacuuming, had left the corner of a rug upturned for Grandmother Koenig to stumble over and fall. The maid, of course, had been dismissed at once—"shown the door"

—and the agency had sent this new one to replace her. She had arrived carrying a plastic cup of coffee for herself, which she had put down on the sideboard. Thus her first task had been to polish this piece of furniture, which she had done in such a way that Grandmother Koenig knew immediately what type of person she was dealing with. "Where do they *find* these people?" she wondered.

Angel interrupted: "Did she help you dress—do your hair—no? Then who helps you?"

"No one," said Grandmother Koenig in a matter-of-fact way, as though it were nothing out of the ordinary that her plum-colored crepe sat on her as smooth as alabaster, nor a hair out of place in her snow-white crown.

But now Angel noticed that she was not quite the same as usual—that in fact she was more spry, and with a gleam in her eyes, which were normally rather stony. She ordered coffee to be brought and then said, "Shut the door, Angelica." She leaned forward: *"She* came to see me." "She," of course, could only be Peter's wife, Lilian. "Nothing to do with this," Grandmother Koenig continued, impatiently indicating the trivial nuisance of her broken arm, "but something quite different. Quite, quite different." She pleasurably tapped her foot in fine double-strapped leather shoe. "Not that she didn't look around to check up on what's there, that's second nature to her, but I saw at once there was something else on her mind . . . I suppose you know about it, Angelica, since the girl is your cousin. I said, 'But why do you come to me?' She said, 'You're his mother.' *Now* she remembers who I am. Put it down," she said to the maid who came in with the coffee tray, "and shut the door behind you." She waited till this was done, but on surveying the tray—"My goodness, can you believe it, *white* sugar, with coffee."

By the time Angel had returned with the correct brown crystals, Grandmother Koenig had passed several stages further into her story: "I didn't tell her in so many words—I was very subtle about it—but I let her know that it wasn't entirely unnatural when the girl is so young and good-looking. Then she asked, 'How do you know?' and when I said I had met her, she really forgot herself: 'What,' she shouted, 'does he always bring his girlfriends to see you?' I said, 'Always?' as though I knew nothing about anything. As though I didn't know my Peter." Here her voice was still light and triumphant, but then it changed: "As though he weren't his father's son."

The gleam had gone from her eyes, giving way to a deeply gloomy look—which may have been the reflection of her dark drawing room, or of the thoughts that had filled her throughout the years she had sat in it. She sighed and compressed her lips: "When I said 'Always?' in that way, I think she would have liked to take it all back, but she couldn't so she went on: 'He's never before set anyone up in a hotel in the middle of New York City.' I understood her better than she thinks; better than I let on."

Angel asked about her arm—wasn't it hurting? How long did they say the cast had to stay on? But her grandmother continued: "That's the worst—when you know everyone knows and have to pretend that nothing is going on. I remember those dinner parties I used to have to give for your grandfather's business friends—your grandfather at the head of the table, entertaining everyone with his stories. At the end of each story he would rap the table with his right hand, the one with the signet ring on his little finger, so then I knew it was time to laugh, I was always the first and then everyone else joined in and sometimes they clapped, first in his direction and then in mine, as if I had said anything witty and as if I didn't know perfectly well what they were all thinking about all the time. It was worst—and this happened too—when it was with the wife of one of his business friends, and she'd be sitting there, laughing at his stories with all the rest, in her décolleté—it was always evening dress, Grandfather insisted on it, everything had to be English—sitting at my table with her naked neck and shoulders for everyone to look at and think what they liked while they laughed and clapped."

"Grandma, Grandma, it's all so long ago!"

But the way Grandmother Koenig had spoken, or the way she looked, wasn't at all like an old person speaking about the dead, but as though it were all still happening and still present to her.

WHEN LARA HEARD about Grandmother Koenig's accident, she wanted at once to visit her. "Who's with her? Just a servant? Oh, she must be so lonely, poor old thing!" She glowed with pity and was ready to leave there and then except she had an appointment with the dentist. She hated these appointments but had to have many of them, for although her teeth were beautiful, they were full of cavities.

Angel went with her and sat in the waiting room, tense with anxiety for everything Lara must be suffering inside. And when Lara emerged, she felt so terrible that Angel had to get a cab to the hotel only two blocks away. Lara took a whole lot of pills to relieve the pain. When Angel asked her what they were, she didn't know though she swallowed them by the handful, throwing them from her palm into her mouth in a quick gesture. They didn't seem to help her much and she continued to lie awake on the bed, suffering from her teeth, devastated. Angel marveled how extreme Lara's emotions were—of pain, joy, or whatever—how completely they took possession of her, so that nothing could allay them till they died down by themselves or were replaced by others, equally intense.

Angel spent as much time with her as she could without neglecting her office work. Not that Lara particularly asked for her company—at this stage she had no difficulty filling the hours she spent alone. She was mostly inside the hotel or in nearby stores. She did a lot of shopping, and Angel's first task on arrival was to admire the new purchases. Lara was especially fond of shoes, and Angel enjoyed watching her stretch out one large but extremely well-formed foot to contemplate a new designer shoe. If she didn't like it, she would take it off and fling it against a wall, not in anger but playfully, blaming herself for her choice. Next day she would return it; she said the clerks in the store knew her very well and laid bets with each other how soon she would come to exchange her purchase. She always got friendly very quickly with the people she met—store clerks or waiters, whomever she happened to come across in the course of her day. For instance, the waiter who serviced her room came in and out very freely and stayed much longer than his duties should have allowed. She asked his opinion along with Angel's on her shopping, or discussed a local event—

murder, kidnap, or jailbreak—seen on television. So she always had people to talk to and didn't seem to need anyone else. She never mentioned any of the students she had met in her drama class, or the teacher either. All that lay behind her in the past, and there was enough in the present to absorb her attention. Of course Peter came whenever he could, entering with an air of absolute possessiveness—which was his right, since he paid the hotel bills. When he arrived, Angel left quickly, although he pretended he wanted her to stay; but Lara took it for granted that it was time for Angel to go. Often she found the room waiter, Roland, outside in the corridor—as soon as he saw Angel he rapped smartly on the door of the adjoining room, pretending he hadn't been loitering outside Lara's.

Very likely, by the time she got home Helena was already in the kitchen—she would appear here in the doorway and tell Angel to go upstairs and wait till dinner was ready. Angel was relieved, she didn't feel like preparing their meal, though she was a good cook, as was her mother, and their arrangement was that whoever was home first would fix dinner. Angel went up to her bedroom, she took her position by her table in the window. It was her favorite time of day, when the lights had come on in all the buildings but whatever was visible of the sky retained some tinge of its own color. Nowadays this sight did not fill her with the strange yet very intimate longing that had made her try to write poetry. Instead, she sat at her table with her head between her hands, full of a different kind of longing—not, like the other, exalting her, but weighing her down, pulling her back. Sometimes it pulled her right back to the hotel. She rushed there in the middle of the night and stood across the street and looked up at the lighted windows stretching to the topmost pinnacle, which was an illuminated pyramid casting its greenish light into the sky.

EVEN WHEN SHE did nothing and went nowhere, Lara gave an impression of intense activity. Probably this was due to her very active mind, which was always churning around new plans, or fragments of plans. These almost invariably had to do with herself. On the rare occasions when she thought about someone else, it was always to brood negatively on that person's character. Lately she had for some reason begun to occupy herself with the Aroras. It may have been a remark of Peter's that had sparked her off, for he was still suspicious that Mrs. Arora was in some way exploiting Helena in their business connection. When Angel, who kept the accounts quite shrewdly, offered to prove to him that this could not be so, he would shrug and say, "Oh, well, maybe not"; yet shortly afterward he might come out again with "Who are these people anyway?" and would want to send in his own accountants.

Overhearing him, Lara must have worked on it in her imagination until one day she was ready to tell Angel about Mrs. Arora: "I didn't trust her from the moment I saw her. She's like a snake; a smiling snake. And I hate the way she touches people—I snatched my hand away and she pretended not to notice and kept on smiling and asked me to call her Mummy. She's sickening. And I'm sure she's a cheat and a thief—all right, Angel, you'll see! You'll remember what I said. She slithers around like someone who's stolen something and is trying to hide it."

Angel knew that Mrs. Arora was hiding something, but that it was far from a theft. Rohit had never mentioned his dead brother again, so that Angel, respecting his silence, had not even asked Helena whether she knew there had been another son besides Rohit. Yet she often thought of this secret and wondered why it should be one.

"And I wouldn't be at all surprised if the son isn't just as bad or worse. Even if he is such a very special friend of yours, Angel. You're too trusting. You have no knowledge of character. That's because you're so inexperienced— you've never been anywhere and you hardly know anyone. What do you think?" she asked—she was standing in front of the mirror, trying out an ivory-colored silk shawl. Angel admired it but Lara impatiently pulled it off again: "You don't know what you're talking about, it makes me look much too pale. You see how I can't trust your judgment in anything, in your eyes every crummy thing is beautiful."

"Yes, if you're wearing it," Angel said stoutly.

"Aren't you sweet," said Lara absently—she was trying the shawl one more time, looking at herself over one shoulder, but, deciding against it finally, she tossed it aside. This annoyance made her forget about the Aroras for the time being, and Angel did not want to revive the subject. Yet she longed to defend Rohit to Lara. She was convinced that if they were better acquainted, they could not fail to appreciate each other.

The next day Rohit came to the office just as she was leaving it. It was not yet five o'clock, and though she used to be punctilious about keeping regular office hours, nowadays she wanted to get to the hotel quickly, before Peter arrived and she had to leave again. Rohit accompanied her

—he tried to talk to her but she was rushing a little ahead of him and sometimes they were separated in the crowd so that he had to work his way around people and hurry to catch up with her. By the time they reached the hotel, both of them were out of breath. They stood under the entrance canopy, where several parties were leaving—sets of suitcases were being wheeled out and stowed away in limousines. Angel and Rohit were in the way, but they continued to stand there a moment longer. She said, "Why don't you come up?" It was not the first time he had accompanied her this far, nor the first time she had asked him in; as always, he refused. She laid her hand lightly on his shoulder —perhaps in a sort of apology—but the next moment she was through the revolving doors. Hurrying over red carpets, past palm trees and marble columns, she didn't even wonder whether he would go home or wander around by himself in the places the two of them used to go together.

"Is he gay?" Lara asked. Rohit might avoid the subject of Lara altogether, but she often spoke of him.

"Oh, no. He's terribly in love with a girl, an airline hostess—"

"What about you and him?"

"Oh, no. Oh, no," disclaimed Angel, laughing.

"Why oh, no?" Lara scrutinized Angel as though she were seeing her for the first time—and actually this was not far from the truth, for Lara did not really see people even when she looked at them. "What do you think of my cousin, Roland?" she asked the room waiter, who was, as so often, hovering around. "Don't you think she's cute?"

Angel laughed out loud at this adjective applied to herself. Roland responded politely, though cursorily, for his glance just swept over Angel before settling back on Lara, who took his admiration for granted or failed to notice it. She returned to Angel: "I don't know why you don't get contact lenses, there's no need at all for those glasses, your grandmother is quite right. How is she, how's her arm? I must go see her again one of these days, though it's very depressing and anyway Peter doesn't want me to, God knows why. He gets some screwy ideas. You know what his latest is?" She stopped, looked at the waiter. "You'd better go, Roland. I'm not sure about tonight, I'll let you know later. He loves taking me to the movies," she explained to Angel. "He knows which ones are good, he reads all the reviews. He's quite intelligent." Although the waiter had left the room, she did not revert to Peter's latest idea but to Rohit: "Have you ever met this airline hostess of his? No? So how do you know she exists? It's so weird, Angel, that two people should be such friends like you and he, and then nothing. Oh, now you're going to ask me what 'nothing' is!" She threw back her head to laugh—her loud, ringing laugh, this time expressing affection: "And *you're* not frigid, are you? I don't think you are;" she playfully drew one finger down Angel's spine, not noticing or caring about the effect she had on her cousin. She soon left off, and returned to the subject of Peter: "I don't understand him, I really don't, I asked him why, when it's so convenient for everyone. Are you listening to me or what, Angel? I hate it when you get that blank look. He wants to buy an apartment, I said fine, and what am I supposed to do there all by myself all day and in the evening when you have to run home to your wife? At least in a hotel there are people to talk to. What it really is, only he won't admit it, an apartment would be cheaper. Well, yes, it would, but he's rich enough, isn't he? Isn't he, Angel? Of course he is—the Koenigs are stinking rich—you're so lucky, Angel, to be coming into Koenig money and not only the ten dollars or whatever we get from the Manarrs."

Both Lara and Angel derived a small income from a trust fund left to them by their grandparents, after the family business had been wound up. In addition, Angel had her salary from Helena, and since she hardly spent anything, she had saved a considerable amount of money to which, until recently, she had never given any thought. But now she did often think of it, with pleasure, and assiduously added to it month by month. She had not yet mentioned this amount to Lara, reserving it for a future contingency of which she had formulated no details except that it would involve them both.

PETER CALLED ANGEL: Grandmother Koenig, just out of plaster, had fallen again and broken the same arm! Angel went immediately and found Peter still there, having just brought his mother back from having her fracture set. She was once more in plaster and there was also a bruise on her forehead, so that, in spite of her perfect toilette, she presented a somewhat battered appearance. She had a guilty look, to have fallen again, but was at the same time defiant, for she and Peter were in the middle of an argument. The maid—and it was still the same one, by some miracle she had lasted several weeks—hovered nearby, anxiously awaiting the outcome of the argument, which was about her. For Peter wanted her to move in with Grandmother Koenig, and she apparently was willing to do this and had already brought her belongings to put into the little room behind the kitchen. Grandmother Koenig maintained she didn't need anyone and that the only reason she had slipped, in the bathroom this time, was that the maid had left some cleaning powder clinging to the tub. She glared at the girl, who smiled humbly and took the hint to withdraw.

"She smokes," Grandmother Koenig told Peter. "She sits in my kitchen and smokes cigarette after cigarette, and when I come in she throws it down the sink and thinks she has fooled me."

Peter made an impatient gesture. He looked to Angel for support and she joined in on his side. The more they reasoned, the more stubborn Grandmother Koenig became. "*And* she drinks, I'm sure. That's why she wants to move in here, because she's in one of those salvation army hostels, where they don't permit alcohol. I refuse to have an alcoholic making herself comfortable in my home." She raised her stately head higher, but when she tried to get up, she tottered a bit and sank back again. Angel rushed to support her, and the maid, who may have been attending through the keyhole, came back to help.

Grandmother Koenig said, "I need only my granddaughter."

"No, Grandma, I can't hold you on my own," Angel said at once, so the maid was permitted to support her from the other side and together they helped her to her bedroom. Here she let them fold back the top lace bedcover but remained fully clothed in her plum crepe. The maid went away, tiptoeing in respect for the air of sanctity that

pervaded the bedroom. Cedar closets as large as antecham-
bers were closed on ranks of stiff long dresses, and the sil-
ver-backed brush, comb, and mirror set was laid out on the
dresser like ceremonial altar pieces. Potpourri and old-fashioned perfumes, a little rotten from congealing, mingled
with the smell of medicines. Grandmother Koenig lay on
the high double bed; on the wall above her was a dark
Spanish celestial scene depicting saints being received by
angels. She allowed Angel to sit by the side of her bed and
hold her large, cold hand.

When she was sure that her grandmother was asleep,
Angel went back to her father. "What shall we do?" she
asked him. But he had already arranged everything with the
girl and had himself carried her suitcase into the maid's
room. She smiled ingratiatingly at Angel, showing her
gums like a little girl with her first milk teeth. Perhaps she
really was or had been an alcoholic or a battered wife; she
appeared helpless, homeless, and wanted very much to stay.
Her name was Rose; she wasn't a girl at all but about forty
years old. "If only Grandmother will let her stay," said
Angel, hoping for both of them.

"She'll have to," said Peter. He had settled it in his
mind. "Or I'll move her out of here and put her in a
retirement place, it's as simple as that." Suddenly angry, he
began to move around the apartment, from one large room
to another. Most of them were tightly sealed, with curtains
drawn, furniture looming in white sheets, wrapped chandeliers hanging down like abandoned apiaries. Peter shook his
head, his nostrils flared, he said several times, "Ridiculous."

"Grandma couldn't live anywhere else," said Angel,
following him.

"Couldn't, couldn't, why couldn't." Peter irritably pushed aside a curtain, but all that became visible was the adjoining building. No inch of space had ever been wasted in this prime location, and whenever enough people had died to vacate the old buildings, these had been swiftly torn down and replaced by tall towers that appeared to be composed entirely of myriads of tiny office windows.

Peter said, "It's not as if she were all that happy here. After Father died." And with a swift glance at Angel: "Or before, if it comes to that . . . They were never an ideal married couple, whatever she might say now."

Angel said, "She doesn't say they were."

He gave her another of his glances: "Oh, she's talked to you, has she? . . . Hmmm. Well. Once upon a time she'd rather have died than uttered a word to anyone, including me. Whatever happened, no one must know, nothing must escape out of these walls. This place always was like a tomb; *she* was like a tomb." He continued to walk around, in agitation now. Angel, following him, knew it was not only at these memories—anything past and gone would not have power to stir him up—but at something else, still alive and happening now. "And why not!" he suddenly exclaimed. "I don't know that it wasn't the better way, people sticking to each other, sticking it out even if everything wasn't one hundred percent perfect."

They had reached the drawing room left open for habitation. He threw himself into a sofa as deep as a bath or a sarcophagus, only to leap up again almost immediately: "I'm not defending my father. I'm not saying he wasn't right till the end a—well, what he had been all his life long. Right till the end," he repeated, but with twitching lips.

"You probably know—only Mother still thinks it's a secret —he died in the traditional way of old men like him, in bed with his latest girlfriend, a real estate agent he'd set up in her own business. Dreadful family disgrace, but except that she tried some hanky-panky with the will—which I soon settled—I don't feel too bad about it. That's the sort of person he was, I'm afraid. It was his nature. You can't blame a person for his nature."

It was in these same words that Grandmother Koenig always absolved Peter of all responsibility for the end of his marriage to Helena. It had ended very swiftly when Helena, on discovering his affair with his dentist's receptionist, had packed up her things that same afternoon and moved herself and Angel back to her parents' house. "A person can't help the nature he's born with," Grandmother Koenig had often explained to Angel, usually ending up, inconsequentially about Helena, "And who does she think she is?"

"Lilian's making a fuss," Peter was saying. "Quite unnecessary, because I don't see that I'm any less with her than I ever was. There've always been late meetings and so on and so forth, but whenever she has one of her dinners, I'm there, she can't say I'm not. She's terribly good with dinners and all of that, which I appreciate, and she enjoys it, too, so what's the point, why throw the whole thing up." He stopped in front of Angel with an air of exasperated righteousness. He was expecting agreement from her, but when it failed to come, he didn't wait for it. Suddenly he seized her arm, he said: "Here, sit down, I want to tell you something." He threw himself next to her on the sofa.

Angel thought he had something very private to say,

but what he confided was: "I'm buying an apartment. Well, why not," he went on immediately, although no one had protested, "it's always a good investment, nothing like real estate." He ran his finger along the back of his collar, and she caught on and said, "Lara likes it in the hotel."

"She says she'll move if you go with her."

He got this in very quickly, as though he had been waiting for the opportunity. When Angel gave no outward sign of reaction, he began to urge her. She could see he wanted it very, very badly. He sat close beside her and cajoled her. She had never expected to see him this way—he always gave an impression of powerful desires but also of being able to satisfy them at will. Now he was dependent on someone else's will, and this was such a new sensation for him that it left him bewildered, and keen like a youth.

She interrupted him to say: "Yes—and Helena?"

He had expected this and was ready for it: "Don't you think you've been her nursemaid long enough—sure you have! If it hadn't been for you, what would have happened to her in all those years when she was incapable of doing anything except lie on her bed and eat? And in all that time I never asked you for one single thing, and what am I asking now except that you should go live with your cousin for a while, just to help her get settled, keep her company, Angel, that's all."

The unaccustomed effort of pleading was hard work for him; he began to perspire and had to take off his jacket. In his shirt-sleeves he looked younger than ever, and he eagerly moved up closer to Angel so that he was like a suitor urging a proposal of marriage. It made her smile, who had never had and did not expect to have such a proposal; and although this was hardly a conventional one, she found herself impatient to accede to it. But still she gave no outward sign, so he felt he had to work harder on her; he perspired more, he undid his top button and loosened his necktie.

Overwhelmed by her father, Angel was relieved when the maid came to tell them that Grandmother Koenig was calling. She jumped up and went into the bedroom, where Grandmother Koenig said plaintively, "I've been calling and calling, and no one heard except her. . . . I want some mint tea." When the maid willingly went off for it, she said, "As if *she'd* know how to make it. No, you don't go," she told Angel. "Stay with me."

She shut her eyes. When Angel stroked her forehead, she did not forbid it. After a while she said, "I don't want her living here."

"Grandma, you need someone, Peter's right, you know he is."

"A stranger off the streets—well, practically—how do we know she doesn't have a disease?"

Angel tried to make a reassuring reply, though her thoughts were elsewhere. She continued to stroke her grandmother's forehead. Stiffly encased in her high-necked dress, Grandmother Koenig lay immobile, her eyes shut. Without opening them, she said: "Why can't *you* come?"

Angel hoped that if she pretended not to have heard this, Grandmother Koenig would be too proud to repeat it. In any case, Angel began frantically to marshal arguments in her mind to prove how impossible it was for her to move in with her grandmother. And it *was* impossible—she realized that she had already absolutely decided on the other course proposed to her. Her heart beat in fear that her grandmother would ask again. When she did not but remained lying silent and even pretending to be asleep, Angel leaned forward gratefully to kiss her forehead with the bruise on it. Never had she loved her grandmother so much as at that moment!

WHEN ANGEL GOT home Mrs. Arora was with Helena. They usually spent the end of the working day in the office together, but now they were upstairs in the living room. Mrs. Arora was on a stool at Helena's feet and Helena was smilingly leaning toward her, her hand in that of Mrs. Arora, who was reading her palm. They formed such a picture of friendship and togetherness that Angel's first thought was well, she's all right now, she doesn't need me anymore.

"Come here, Angel!" Helena's broad, middle-aged face beamed at her. She wanted Mrs. Arora to read Angel's palm too. For her it was a joke, but Mrs. Arora was so serious that Angel, who disliked such dabblings, was reluctant to hold out her hand. Helena insisted, wanted it very much, till Angel sat next to her and gave her hand to be read. Mrs. Arora bent over it, and Helena put her arm around Angel's shoulders, hugging them in anticipation of the happy fortune about to be revealed.

Mrs. Arora's forefinger crept slowly around and around Angel's palm. But in spite of Helena's impatient queries, she remained silent. Angel looked down on Mrs. Arora's coiffure; the finger roaming around her palm felt like an insidious insect. She could not help recall Lara's dark hints: no, she did not believe them. Helena was prompting,

"What about love and marriage? Oh, all right, then what about being very rich and famous?" Mrs. Arora promised nothing, slowly drawing her finger along the lines of fate inscribed in Angel's palm.

"What's the use if you can't promise *any*thing," Helena grumbled; she pretended to be joking but sounded genuinely disappointed. Angel was glad to withdraw her hand, and as she did so, she suddenly met Mrs. Arora's eyes fixed on her. They held a strange expression, and she quickly lowered them, as though they had exposed something that she wanted to keep hidden. For a moment Angel was not sure whether this something was what could be read in the lines of her palm, or whether it was a secret in Mrs. Arora's own life, but decided at once that it must be the latter.

Later Angel asked Helena, "Did you know she had another son, who died?"

"Yes, but that's all I know. She never speaks of him. Has Rohit told you anything? No, I guess it's just too terrible for them. . . . And probably that's why they're so close— I've never seen a mother and grown-up child so all in all to each other. It's like you and I used to be." She was plumping up some cushions, and this activity enabled her to slip in the last sentence incidentally and, if so desired, inaudibly. She went on at once: "She thinks about Rohit all the time. She knows where he is every minute of the day, what he's doing, who he's with, who are his friends. . . . She's very sorry you and he are no longer as friendly as before."

Angel said, "Who told her that?"

"But, darling, that's what I mean—she doesn't have to be told, she just knows! The same way I just know about you." She plumped the same cushion for the third time.

"There's not that much to know about me." Angel laughed lightly, but at the same time she was calculating whether this was a good time to tell Helena about moving out of the house. She realized how uncharacteristic, indeed incongruous, it was for her to calculate anything—and especially with regard to her mother. But she accepted it as part of her new circumstances. Once everything had been simple; Angel herself had been simple. But now there was an involvement—a responsibility toward another—that made her complex and, when necessary, devious.

PETER BOUGHT THE apartment in Angel's name, thereby securing himself all around: for no one could challenge his right to make such a gift to his own daughter, and also he himself was satisfied that nothing was going out of the family. It was in a brand-new building, in a part of the city that was exploding with expensive real estate ventures. These were all in various states of incompletion so that throughout the day the streets quaked with the roar of heavy machinery tearing up the earth. The sidewalks were boarded off, and at lunchtime workmen squatted in rows against the boards with their giant Pepsis and hero sandwiches. The building into which Peter had bought was almost finished, and many of the apartments had been sold —mostly to foreigners needing their own space in the city for their dealings with it. There were Japanese businessmen moving in shoals, and stout blond Israelis who ran around on short legs with speed and purpose. All these people were furnishing their new apartments, criss-crossing with the workmen who were still painting them. The lofty entrance lobby of black glass was in constant flux, and much of its traffic may have gone unchecked in spite of the receptionists, as earnest as spacemen, manning the high-tech security system.

Peter had bought an apartment on a very high floor, and it had windows all the way around so that it hung suspended amid the topmost branches—the cliffs and towers—of the city. It was thrilling by day and in a different way by night, and Lara was deeply thrilled by her possession of it. She didn't know and it wasn't worth telling her that it was in Angel's name—that was only a technicality, for obviously it really belonged to Lara. They went to view it several times before moving in, and she ran from room to room, window to window, while Peter and Angel followed her, their footsteps echoing stolidly through the empty space; never had they been as united as now, when they felt themselves to be the necessary anchors to her soaring spirits.

At first Lara planned to buy a lot of furniture, and there were some excited shopping expeditions. But then she changed her mind and canceled what she had ordered; one Plexiglas tea trolley had already reached the service entrance, but she refused to accept delivery because she said she just wanted space—to dance in perhaps, but principally to *be*. She stretched in a yearning way, yearning to expand —"You're laughing at me!" she accused Peter and Angel but she laughed herself, and her strange eyes swam.

So it happened that when she moved in, it was into an almost empty space with only a few rugs, cushions, and a record player in the living room and a futon and dresser in each of the two bedrooms. One of these bedrooms was meant for Angel, although there had been no discussion about her moving in with Lara. But from the very first night, when Peter had to go home to his wife, it was clearly impossible to leave Lara alone. It was even impossible to leave her alone in her bedroom—Angel did start off on the other futon, but it wasn't long before Lara called to her that she was lonely, missing Peter, and anyway felt odd in a new place. So Angel got in with her and held her till Lara fell asleep.

Angel's days were spent as before, in the basement office conscientiously running her end of Helena's business. This gave both her and her mother the opportunity to pretend that nothing had changed. Helena played her part with more spirit than Angel: perhaps because she had to work harder at it, to appear cheerful and unhurt in the face of Angel's superabundant happiness—and her obvious indifference to what she had left behind. Although Angel was in the house every working day, there were times when she never left the basement, as though the rest of the house no longer existed for her. Sometimes she had to go upstairs to her own room to collect some more things she needed to take away with her; but she never lingered, never glanced out the window at which she had spent so many hours, never opened the drawer in which her poems lay.

THE EXCITEMENT OF having a new place—new space—a new beginning stayed with Lara for some time. When neither Peter nor Angel could be there, she kept herself busy on her own and did not complain of their absence. They were not sure what it was she did to fill the day, but in any case it appeared for the moment to satisfy her. She slept late, and then she hung around in the lobby, where she made friends with the young receptionists in the same way as she had with the people in the hotel. That was her way: she appeared to have no friends or acquaintances carried over from the past but to make new ones wherever she went. However, while dropping people with the same nonchalance as she took them up, she accepted them if they chose to reappear. For instance, when Roland, her waiter from the hotel, began to spend his time off with her, she took this so entirely for granted that she didn't bother to mention it to Peter and Angel. Each of them, on separate occasions, was surprised to see him with her: Angel, returning from the office, discovered Roland cooking pasta in the kitchen, while Peter came upon him one afternoon squatting with Lara on the floor of the empty living room, figuring out a pack of tarot cards.

Lara called Angel in the office several times a day—not for anything specific to say but picking up the phone because it was there and Angel readily available at the other end. She usually lost interest quite soon and hung up. But after some time these calls became more purposeful. Angel recognized that they were no longer the result of Lara having nothing better to do, but were a stage in what she was doing: this was brooding on various wrongs and the people who had caused them. At a certain level of indignation she snatched up the telephone and launched at once into the middle of her own thought process. Often it took Angel some time to catch on—as when Lara said one day, "I'm convinced they work as a team." It wasn't until she said "I'm not even sure that they're mother and son" that Angel realized she was talking about the Aroras. Rohit happened to be in the office on an errand, so she couldn't even defend him and his mother as vigorously as she would have liked. She hunched herself over the phone and said several times, "Lara, no," and in the end hung up much more quickly than she really wanted to. Rohit, with his abnormal sensitivity, knew himself to have been the subject of the conversation, so that, avoiding each other's eyes, they both talked quickly and at unnecessary length about the business on which he had been sent.

Although usually Lara had forgotten her grievance by the time Angel got home, on that day Peter had arrived just after Angel had hung up too quickly so that Lara had shared her suspicions about the Aroras with him. It was not in Peter's character to leave anything unresolved; and as soon as Angel came in, he said, "I've said time and time again, who *are* these people: don't you think we should find out?"

"You know what you're like," Lara told Angel. "You may be sitting there in that office all day, thinking you know what's going on, and meanwhile they're just laughing at you and robbing you blind."

Angel knew herself to be more shrewd than Lara was giving her credit for; she also knew that Lara wasn't speaking literally but emotionally, out of the dark web she had spun inside her head during her hours of having nothing to do.

But Peter, whose understanding was strictly literal, was already at the telephone: "I'm going to speak to Helena right now."

"She's not home," Angel said. She hoped he wouldn't ask where she was, but he did, so she had to tell him that probably she was with the Aroras. She knew they usually saw to it that Helena did not have to spend her evenings alone.

Peter frowned: "Are those people hanging around there day and night?"

But Lara was tired of the subject of the Aroras. She announced that she was going to dance—and at once began to go up and down the empty space. She presented some movements of classical ballet and some of what she had picked up of Indian dance forms, so she was alternately stamping out an exotic rhythm with her feet and waving her arms around as a softly dying swan. It wasn't different from her performance as a child—"Now I'm a flower!" "Now a princess!" "See the deer!"—she still moved heavily and did not use her abundant energy in the right way, so she was soon out of breath. It didn't matter, her audience of two enjoyed her performance and enormously applauded her.

Although she was usually asleep when Angel left for the office, the next morning Lara suddenly appeared from her bedroom. She was not in a good mood. She didn't want Angel to go to the office—not that she particularly desired her company, it was her allegiance to the office, to Helena, to the Aroras, to what she called that whole setup that angered her. Unwilling to argue, Angel wanted only to calm Lara. As always at such moments, she was afraid of and for her cousin. She was even ready to give her the pills of which Lara had such a large and varied stock; but when she offered to fetch them, Lara replied harshly that she knew when she was sick and didn't need Angel to tell her, although perhaps it suited Angel to tranquilize her out of existence. Angel, who had been about to leave, took off her jacket and put away her purse and asked Lara if she could make coffee for her.

"No," Lara said. "No, I don't want anything. Except I don't want you to go to that office. Oh, I know what's going on. Don't think I don't. Get me some orange juice. Please," she added irritably, and padded on naked feet into the bathroom. When Angel followed her with the juice, Lara already had some pills in the palm of her hand; she threw back her head and swiftly swallowed them.

Lara went back into her bedroom but Angel waited outside. She hoped Lara would call for her but did not go in for fear of irritating her. Cacophonous street sounds pierced unfiltered all the way up to their floor—police sirens, electric drills, the fevered bellow of an ambulance. Angel's attention was strained entirely toward the bedroom. At last Lara called her—she was sitting amid the crumpled sheets of her futon on the floor, still in her nightdress, which had slipped off one shoulder; this made her look not wanton but slovenly.

"Peter told me about you and Helena. How selfish she's been, making you look after her all the years you went to school and even now—yes!" She flared up at the smallest sign of denial from Angel, "Peter told me all about it, so don't lie to me."

Angel kept quiet, and after a while she was rewarded by Lara calling to her in a melting voice: "Come here. Sit here. With me." Angel got down beside her in her sea of flowered sheets. Lara straightened Angel's collar, and said, "It's for you, for your sake I'm saying it. Because I'm here to look after you now. It's nothing to laugh at," she mock-frowned, but Angel couldn't help laughing; it was so absurd and delightful to think of Lara looking after *her*.

"I suppose you think you're much cleverer than me, and sensible and practical and all," Lara carried on in the same warm, teasing tone, still straightening Angel's collar but now also letting her fingers play against her neck. "But there are some things I know about that you don't." Her whole hand was laid around Angel's neck. "Because you're so innocent; so goddamn trusting; so goddamn stupid sometimes."

"Don't, Lara," Angel said, for now Lara's thumb was pressing against her windpipe.

"Don't, Lara what? Don't tell the truth of what's really going on? She shouldn't be running an office in the house. She shouldn't even be living in the house. It's not hers. Oh, am I choking you? Sorry, darling, Lara's sorry." She made conciliatory kissing sounds and let go.

"Not entirely," she continued. "It's not hers entirely. It belongs to all of us."

"Well, to her and Hugo," Angel said.

"That means all of us. That means you and me, Angel. It's our family house really, isn't it, our grandparents left it to us so she shouldn't be just keeping it for herself. Also it's ridiculous that only one person should be in that whole place; it's insane. We should be selling it." She compressed her lips on that last statement, but at the same time her eyes swam toward Angel, light eyes under dark lashes.

"Maybe you're right," Angel said, speaking in a measured way. "Probably you are. But somehow, I don't know why not, we've never thought of it."

"Don't you think we should," said Lara quite gently and humbly, leaving it all to Angel to reflect on and decide.

THE SUBJECT OF the house did not disturb Angel too much, for she knew that Lara might feel terribly strongly about something one day, only to forget about it the next, at least temporarily. But when on the following afternoon Hugo showed up in the office, she guessed the purpose of his visit; and cutting through his embarrassed preliminaries, she asked if Lara had spoken to him about selling the house. He admitted it apologetically: "She gets these ideas, it doesn't really mean anything to her. We wouldn't want Helena to sell the house—why should she? She needs it for herself, and for you if you decide you have to move back." He went on in a rush: "Don't think I don't appreciate it, what you're doing—"

"What am I doing?" asked Angel in surprise.

"I know what living with her is like," he replied. "Oh, yes, she can be wonderful, great company, but she can also be—absolute hell," he concluded in a lowered voice, but in any case Angel had already interrupted him:

"She's wonderful all the time." She began to lisp, tripping over her tongue in excitement. "And when she's not, it's only because of something that's happened or not happened, it's only a mood—every one of us has moods sometimes, everyone in the world, it'd be unnatural if we didn't."

"You sound like your father," Hugo said. "Peter's always telling me—on the phone, he won't see me—'It's natural, old chap, perfectly human and natural.' He has absolutely no idea what he's doing. As far as he's concerned, every desire is natural and therefore permissible. Every desire of his, that is. He's like an animal. No, not like, he is. He *is* an animal." Hugo checked himself. When he spoke again, it was as near to his usual flippant manner as he could make it: "Does he still read funny books very slowly? I used to see him with the same *Carry On, Jeeves* for months on end. Still? And still *Carry On, Jeeves?* And he's the one with the literary daughter, and I've got Lara. Not literary? But at least you read and you write poetry, or used to. . . . Did you know that Lara has read nothing, not a word of anything I've written? It's not only that she's not interested, it's a principle with her."

"Lara doesn't read too many books."

"What's she do all day?" Hugo asked, as if casually.

"Oh, she does such a lot! She buys things—and then she takes them back—and she meets friends—"

"Does she have any?"

"She has me," smiled Angel, but followed up at once with "She has *masses* of friends—you know how she is, talking to everyone she meets, and they all adore her." After only the slightest pause she asked, "Why does she take those pills?"

"Does she take a lot of them?"

"I don't know what she takes when I'm not there. I'd better ask her." Angel assumed an air of innocence, pretending to believe that Lara would tell her the truth.

Hugo suggested, "You could search around a bit and see what she has and how much."

Angel promised she would, not letting on that she had already very thoroughly done so.

ANGEL SAW HER mother every working day, but weekends she devoted to Lara, so that sometimes she didn't even have time to call Helena. When she did, Helena always pretended to be having such a full and entertaining weekend that Angel was not missed at all; but as the conversation drew to a close, she became more wistful, and more tense about not asking what Angel unfortunately could not offer. Lara waited for Angel to finish to ask, "What did she want? Oh, don't tell me nothing, she wants you to come there." She stared at Angel, daring her to say that she wanted to go; but behind that challenge crouched something small and desperate that pleaded not to be left alone.

Peter, of course, spent the weekend at his home in the river suburb, so it was left entirely to Angel to do what she could to entertain Lara. When she suggested a movie or a concert, Lara agreed, but in the end she either wouldn't go or, if she did, soon got bored or, more often, upset—maybe by someone breathing too loudly in the row behind, or by some smell, or just something in the atmosphere was uncongenial. She and Angel spent much time in the streets among the idle holiday crowd who trailed past the windows of the big stores, or bargained for stolen goods with sidewalk entrepreneurs on the alert for the police. By late Sunday afternoon the city wore an air of stale disappointment. Dealers who had kept open their lost-our-lease discount stores could be seen sitting alone amid their unsold stock.

Derelicts filled their sacks from the corner trash containers overflowing with battered soft–drink cans.

At the end of one such aimless weekend Lara decided she wanted to go see where Peter lived. "Only from out-side," she said. She was on a sudden spurt of willful energy and seemed prepared to go alone, so Angel knew she would have to go with her. When they arrived at Grand Central, it was deserted, for it was too late to leave the city and too early to come back. Under the grandiose vault, lit up by Beaux Arts lamps, candy wrappers and other bits of paper blew about. A few homeless people sat modestly behind pillars, where they would not be noticed too much, and a lonely man was the only customer at the lunch counter, ignored by the waitress fixing her hair in the mirror. Lara's high heels echoed through the empty marble hall in a defi-ant marching rhythm that made it clear she would not turn back.

It was only forty-five minutes to Peter's station, and here a young cab driver took charge of them. He said he was lucky to have found them, for it was not usual to get passengers off the later Sunday trains, and by this time he was normally resigned that his weekend earnings were at an end. He drove with one hand, the other laid along the back of the seat as he turned around to talk to and get a good look at them. Angel was supposed to know the way to Peter's house, but she kept getting them lost. She had never paid attention when she had come here as a child, having had to concentrate too hard on not giving way to her homesickness, which had started the moment she stepped off the train. Unaided by her, it was their driver who found the house. They approached it from an undulation planted with a copse of trees, and it opened before them in a bird's-eye view: Peter and Lilian's house, a white Romanesque villa with an arched porch. A lawn spread in front and to one side, and on the other side was a tennis court and at the back a swimming pool of heavenly blue. It was all as empty as an architect's perspective, and even the swimsuits spread out to dry on the deck chairs by the pool were like simulated effects of habitation. "Where *are* they?" asked Lara in such disappointment that Angel suspected she had after all intended to go in and confront them. The driver was now completely turned around in his seat, a member of their party, ready to drive them anywhere.

Lara said she wanted to go find them. Angel objected how was it possible with no idea where they might be— though in fact she had a pretty good idea that they were having drinks followed by early Sunday supper in any one of a dozen family homes in the neighborhood. Peter and Lilian's weekends were not aimless or unstructured but moved from tennis to brunch or cocktail parties, unless there was a bigger event like a charity gala in the empty airplane hangar. Angel suggested catching the next train back, but instead of going to the station their driver continued around the leafy country roads winding between trees in bloom. There were occasional glimpses of idyllic residences set well back from the road and from each other; no human beings were in sight, only sometimes a golden retriever barked from behind a wrought iron gate. The driver apologized for every bump in the road and the state of his sedan, for which he blamed the old woman who owned it. He was just her employee, he told them, and only till he could find something better. He hadn't lived in the place

long and couldn't wait to get out. Probably it was fine for
the people in the white houses with the trees and grass, but
the rest of the town was just this dump with no jobs and no
place to rent.

Now they were driving along the river, where little
white sailboats skimmed on the water, and others bobbed at
anchor by the shore. The driver said that he himself had
been lucky, he had a friend who let him stay with him in
his apartment, though it was just a hole with no furniture
and one night he had seen a rat this big—he took his hands
off the wheel to show how big, and Lara screamed. He
turned up a side street ascending steeply from the river and
then more steeply up another street, and here the ruined
clapboard houses started with peeled-off paint and presumably rats in them (it was being near the water, their driver
said). He stopped outside a bar which had limp cotton curtains in the window screening off whatever might be going
on inside. The young man invited them to join him for a
drink—Angel would have liked to take the next train
home, but it was not possible, for the way he invited them
was so modest and so hopeful, though with a smile that
already understood he might be turned down.

Inside it was cramped and gloomy with old-fashioned
furnishing—not only the curtains but the revolving barstools with cracked leather seats and the ranks of booths
that could be curtained off. The jukebox and the cigarette
machine were both nickel-plated antiques and only the clientele was young—especially the girls with their short skirts
out of which emerged endless long white legs. They gave
out a feminine odor masked by sweet perfumes, and this
mixture lay in an oddly fresh way on top of the ingrained

smell of beer and potato chips. Their escort ushered Lara
and Angel past the barstools—the room was so narrow they
had to walk single file—and settled them in the end booth.
Having asked permission to call his friend to join them, he
walked over to the wall telephone, sedate and content with
himself, a man entertaining two lady friends. Lara fished
out her compact and examined her teeth for lipstick marks;
she winked at Angel in amused anticipation. When the
young man rejoined them, he, too, gave out an air of anticipation, and so did his friend, who arrived remarkably
quickly, his hair still wet where he had hurriedly slicked it
down.

Although their escorts were a few years younger than
Angel and Lara, they gave an impression of maturity, as if
they had already passed through many scenes of life. Both
tried to be gallant but were stiff with shyness, even their
driver, who had been so voluble before. His friend was
small and thin with almost a child's undeveloped physique;
he kept his eyes lowered into his beer, only flicking an
occasional upward glance at Lara. When he spoke, his voice
came out rusty with nervousness and he quickly relapsed
into silence. But Lara was happy to do all the talking. She
was at her best. She was drinking a very sweet cocktail and
this may have helped raise her spirits; but mostly it was a
determination to be lively—there was usually a willfulness
about her moods, which were never quite spontaneous.
Now, after her disappointing day, she was prepared to pour
out her personality on these two new shy admirers and
overwhelm them with herself. She tossed back her hair, and
every now and again as she talked she gently touched their
hands with her brilliant fingernails. She radiated beyond

their booth, so that people craned around from the bar to get a look at her and even the leggy girls sometimes stopped their own laughter to listen to hers. The two young men were still somewhat rigid with shyness as they drank in her every word and jingle from her golden bracelets; they left their hands immobile on the table, in case she wanted to touch them again.

When she told them she was a dancer, the driver asked, "What sort of dancer?" with suppressed excitement though trying to sound calm. She explained to them, and this was the best part for Angel. It seemed so long since Lara had talked about being a dancer, as if she had laid this ambition aside. Now she spoke of it with passion: not in its peripheral aspect of lessons, studios, and dance teachers, but what it meant to her, to her self, and she indicated this as both the highest point of expression of her personality and its negation insofar as she ceased to be Lara and was now a flower, now a tiger, now a deer resting in the shade. The young men were impressed, and even if they didn't fully understand what she meant, they recognized it to be noble and beautiful. Lara indicated Angel—"And my cousin is a poet," to which Angel assented with a smile, glad and willing to contribute to the exalted atmosphere Lara had created.

Now it was the turn of the two young men. Yes, said the driver, he was living in this hole and driving a beat-up sedan he was ashamed to have people sit in, but soon he was going to have things straightened out. It was just that he was passing through a bad time, was down on his luck, it could happen to anyone if you were poor, which was an occasion for everyone to dump on you. The friend nodded, it was his story too—that was how they had met, the driver admitted candidly, in a house of correction, where they both ended up through no fault you could call their own. It wasn't a jail, more a camp, you wore these fatigues like the army and did healthy outdoor work, but still you felt pretty bad, humiliated, especially when you were out working on the roads and people passed you in their cars. The friend had been let out first and he had come to this town where he had an uncle who found him work doing deliveries for one of the big supermarkets in the mall. It might not sound like much, the driver said, but better than riding around in that old sedan, which must be about the worst job in the world—you hung around by the station and all these people got off and drove away in their own expensive foreign cars, and if you were in luck, you ended up with a couple of teenage students who had smashed up their own cars and sent them for repairs. With clientele like that, you can forget about tips, but try and explain that to the old woman who owned the sedan—and at mention of his employer he made a big effort to control his feelings. No, he said, he was going to keep quiet till he was ready to quit, and even then on no account would he let himself be provoked. That was how he had gotten in trouble before, but now he knew himself better, knew his own strength and weaknesses. He looked down at his hands lying on the table—big, powerful hands, which might get out of control; he turned them around, peering at the lifelines, unable to read them. He had always been good with his hands, he said, he had a natural talent for carpentry, and in the camp they had promised him a training course, only the papers never came through. But the moment he had a decent job, he would study in the evenings and pay for it himself; and his friend was going to learn restoration work so he could fix up old junk and sell it for fantastic prices. Because he had this incredible ability with *his* hands—and now they all looked at the friend's hands, which had bad fingernails but were girlishly slender and lily-white. They would have a company—carpentry and restoration—and at last would earn some proper money like everyone else which they badly needed: especially the friend whose wife was after him for child support and was threatening to have him locked up again. They had both been married—the driver's wife had disappeared long ago, gone to live in another state, but the friend had two kids he had to make these monthly payments for. Two boys, Kevin and Marvin, aged five and four; they had had them over for Christmas when their mother had gone off on a binge with her sister. The driver had cut down a Christmas tree and brought it home at night on top of the sedan; and they had put little toys that kids like under it and had decorated it with lights and all sorts of stars and angels that had gone on sale at the supermarket after midnight on Christmas Eve. The bar had become very crowded now, and there was a tune on the jukebox that had been popular some years earlier. The four of them all knew it and loved it and moved to the beat, remembering when it had first come out, which must have been about the time when Kevin and Marvin were conceived and Lara had been taking dancing lessons and Angel writing poetry.

They were nearly too late for the last train and had to make a dash for the station. The driver assured them that if they missed it, he and his friend would drive them all the way to the city in the old woman's sedan and the next day he would quit the job. But they didn't miss it—they could hear it as they drove up and they ran into the station with no time to buy their tickets and no time even to offer to pay the driver (which saved embarrassment, for he would never have taken their money). This last Sunday-night train was packed and there were no seats, so Angel and Lara had to stand in the space between the carriages just outside the women's toilet. It was night and they couldn't see much outside, only a ghostly reflection from the sky in the river and a few mysterious points of light scattered over the dark hills. The passengers swayed to and fro with the motion of the train, and many of them were lulled to sleep. They looked blissful as at the end of a weekend where every nice thing had happened. After a while Angel and Lara were too tired to stand and they slid to the floor; Lara fell asleep, and she, too, was smiling like the other sleeping passengers. Angel put her arm around her so that her head could be supported on Angel's shoulder, and it was a happy journey in spite of the discomfort of the floor and women having to step over their legs to get in and out of the toilet.

3

THE NEXT TIME Angel visited her grand-
mother—unfortunately she was no longer able to go there
as often as was probably necessary—Grandmother Koenig
was out of plaster; the bruises on her face had faded and she
appeared to be almost herself.

"Shut the door!" she shouted at the maid, Rose, whom
she suspected of trying to pry into her private affairs. It was
true that Rose tended to hover, but apparently more out of
concern than curiosity. She made secret signs to Angel behind Grandmother Koenig's back, to indicate her employer's state of health and mind; also that she would like to
talk to Angel privately herself, and Angel hoped she would
be able to manage this before the end of her visit. Meanwhile, however, Grandmother Koenig monopolized her in
the drawing room, with the doors shut against Rose.

"Peter hasn't been to visit me for two weeks. Where is he? Is he still with that cousin of yours? Well, that's not *my* business—it's for his wife to think about—but at least he could remember his mother sometimes." Grandmother Koenig sat as upright as ever on her hugely upholstered sofa. It was her voice that appeared to have changed—or perhaps it was only a change of tone, from righteous indignation commanding assent to a querulousness pleading for attention. Suddenly she ducked her head, and in what was for her a whisper—"Open the door—she's listening there—"

"No, Grandma, no—and even if she were—"

Grandmother Koenig's head went up again, swaying its proud coiffure. "What sort of manners is that, to listen at the door? No decently brought up person would dream of doing such a thing." She fixed Angel with a stare that had once been like flint but was now blurred by weak vision. And the next moment she herself became weak, again querulously questioning, "Why do I have to have such a person in my home when you could come to be with me? Your mother can spare you for a time, why is she so selfish when she knows I haven't been well and need my granddaughter to help me—she *is* listening," Grandmother Koenig interrupted herself and called out: "Rose!"

The double doors slid open at once and between them stood Rose, smiling and making no pretence that she had not been listening. "Should I bring your tea now?"

"We don't want tea. We want you to shut the door and go away into the kitchen and wait there until you're called." Grandmother Koenig spoke firmly but not unkindly, and Rose, still smiling, did as she was told.

Grandmother Koenig fell into a mood of nostalgia: "In my grandmother's house the maids always curtsied. Of course we don't expect it today—certainly not, I'm not so behind the times, and what's it mean anyway, even if it is gracious. . . . She's not a bad girl, at least she tries and is willing though stupid. But what can you expect, she's had no education to speak of, and no money at all, ever." This last she spoke in a wondering tone, as of something too bizarre for human understanding. "I let her sit with me in the evenings—she talks too much but sometimes it's quite interesting. She's told me such extraordinary things, Angelica, who would have dreamed such things could happen to people? I think she must be making it up—but not all of it, surely no human being could make all that up? She drinks a little bit, but then, I have to say I've never had anyone in my kitchen who could keep out of the cooking sherry. She's definitely not an alcoholic, not like her mother was." She began to tell some of Rose's story: besides the alcoholic mother, there were sexual assaults by a stepfather, and a teenage marriage to a sadist who was jailed for causing her grievous bodily harm. Grandmother Koenig spoke in a voice hushed with awe, as one recounting a fantastic fable or some such otherworldly tale.

Angel listened and made the right responses, but she was also intent on her grandmother, trying to gauge where and what was the change in her, and was it in her or in her surroundings? Both seemed the same—Grandmother Koenig encased in her crepe dress, and the room muffled in rugs laid on top of the carpet. Maybe the only change was that such stories as Rose's should have penetrated in here and into the mind of Grandmother Koenig, who was telling them. But then Angel noticed that there was a stain on her grandmother's dress, a food stain that must have been there a long time, for it was already so deeply ingrained into the fabric that it would be forever impervious to the dry cleaner. And was it Angel's imagination, or did the congenitally dark drawing room now appear dimmed as well, as though the chandeliers had gathered a film of dust on all their crystal drops and hangings? Angel secretly imitated a gesture she had often seen her grandmother make—she drew her finger along the chair on which she sat, though immediately wiping it off on her skirt without giving herself the chance to notice that it was full of dust.

Something else uncharacteristic happened that day: Grandmother Koenig fell asleep before the end of Angel's visit. She continued to sit bolt upright on her sofa, but her eyes were shut and her mouth had dropped open. Angel went to look for Rose, to help her put Grandmother Koenig to bed, and found her in her maid's room behind the kitchen. It was as narrow as a closet, with only a bed, a chair, and a table, all very plain, but Rose had made herself most comfortable. She was sitting at the table with a cigarette and a very full ashtray and was pouring herself a drink from a bottle which was not cooking sherry but an excellent Scotch. It was all right about Grandmother Koenig, she assured Angel; every evening she dropped off this way and then she woke up again and let Rose help her get ready for bed. Rose would bring her supper on a tray, and she always sat with her for a while and they had some nice talks. The moment Grandmother Koenig was in her nightie, she became girlish and clinging, a changed personality.

"She doesn't want me to leave her alone though she's

too proud to say it," Rose said. "But I can see she wants me
to sit with her and I like to do it and let her talk a bit."

Rose drank and smoked; her white, worn little face
looked rested. On the wall above the bed she had hung one
picture, of Jesus with soft eyes and a golden beard. "She's
had a dog's life, if you'll excuse me saying that about your
grandma, and about your grandpa about who the less said, I
guess, the better. And in a beautiful home like this, with all
that money in the bank, you'd think people would *have* to
be happy, why wouldn't they be? But no, that's not what
we're here for, I've learned that much, not for our own
pleasure but for eternal misery all around," sighed Rose
deeply out of her deep contentment.

PETER CALLED ANGEL and asked her to come over
to his office. She was surprised, for he had never before
asked her to meet him there—in fact, she had never been to
this office into which he had moved a few years before,
after taking over as chairman of his family firm. Unlike the
old office, which had been in an elaborate landmark building of the twenties, this new one was in a complex of
superstructures put up after a great deal of controversy and
was regarded by some as a marvel and by others as a mon-
ster of modern architecture. The lobby was as busy as a
traffic intersection, and there were so many elevators taking
off to so many floors and into ever higher regions that
Angel took the wrong one and had to get off at an interme-
diary landing—as blank and deserted as the moon—and
wait to be taken down again. Peter's own office was the
highest on the floors belonging to his firm. It was space

pure and simple, space for its own sake, with furnishing like abstract sculpture—some of it *was* abstract sculpture—enclosed in a sheath of glass that did nothing to section it off from the extension of space into which it was inserted. The staggering view was not so much of a city as of an intricately constructed engineering model, with river and park sketched in at appropriate places.

It was in this up-to-the-minute expression of metropolitan might that Peter told Angel the sad little story of the Arora family. He had had them investigated by a private agency whom he knew to be reliable, having often used them in the course of his business affairs. They had soon discovered that the Aroras had not come to New York because of Rohit's job and his mother's business, but that these opportunities had been created to let them get away from their family scandal in India. This was on account of Rohit's elder brother—"But he died," said Angel quickly, as if she wished not to have to hear any more. "Yes, he died," said Peter, making a distasteful face, as if he wished not to have to tell any more; "of stab wounds in a prison brawl."

He had been in prison for five years. The first three were taken up by the trial and the last two by appeals against his death sentence. These had all been rejected, and at the time he died he was awaiting the result of his petition for mercy to the President—which was in fact turned down, and his two accomplices had been hanged. Like himself, they had been students at the university, wild young men who were always in need of more money than their families were able to provide. Full of adventurous spirits and urgent desires, the young men had used their superior intelligence to work out a scheme of robbing an armored van on its way from a bank vault. But in spite of their ingenious planning, some trifling detail of timing had gone wrong, and in no mood to be thwarted, they had drawn their guns, hitherto used only on seasonal pigeon shoots. A guard had been killed and, during the ensuing pursuit, a policeman; then it was all up with the three students, and the lives of their families were shattered.

Peter didn't want Lara to be told about this. He said she was too—"Nervous. Or whatever," he said, waving his hand at this, for him, unaccustomed and therefore uncomfortable concept. Anyway, his first instinct was to shield her, and normally it would have been Angel's too: but for once her mind did not immediately spring to Lara but to Rohit and his mother. She felt she had failed them in friendship in never discerning the abyss that lay beneath the surface of the lives they shared with herself and Helena. Peter thought she ought to tell Helena; it was his opinion that financial partners should be in complete possession of all personal and other information about each other. Angel did not argue with him; she was too overwhelmed by these facts to be capable of deciding how to deal with them.

It so happened that when she returned to the office, Mrs. Arora was there with Helena. They had just finished going over their order schedules, and now Mrs. Arora was trying to persuade Helena to accompany her and Rohit to an Indian wedding party that evening. Helena was reluctant and Mrs. Arora was coaxing her in that soft, sweet, insinuating way she had. "Don't you think she should come? Make her come," she pleaded with Angel, and she touched Angel's shoulder in what was partly a caress and partly massage—and yet was tentative enough to be withdrawn instantly, at the slightest hint of a recoil.

WHEN ROHIT FOUND Angel waiting for him outside his airline office, he was extraordinarily pleased. It was like old times, when she had often come to meet him and they walked home together. Now, too, they walked eastward toward Helena's house, in the opposite direction from where Angel had gone to live with Lara. Rohit talked away happily about all sorts of things he thought would interest her. Since it was the evening rush hour, they moved with one tide of people and against another, so they were often swept apart; moreover, buses, cars, trucks, and moving vans, jam-packed in the street, braked and shrieked so that most of what Rohit was saying got swallowed up. All this worked in Angel's favor, for it prevented Rohit from noticing her lack of attention. She had not yet made up her mind whether she would mention his brother or not; her purpose in coming was not entirely clear to her except she wanted to be with him in a reaffirmation of their friendship.

They walked toward the East River, and after negotiating the last avenue of snarled traffic, they were in a quieter place. Here the phalanx of high-rise buildings was momentarily broken by a row of family houses, gracious in red brick and with white shutters. They abutted on an enclosed courtyard-like space, where a fountain flowed from a stone St. Bernard dog, mostly visited by the elegant children of diplomats and their nannies. A row of benches set into the parapet enclosing this little park overlooked the river, which was dotted with barges and pleasure boats. The usual dense and ceaseless traffic flowed under the parapet, with a muffled roar that didn't sound too different from the surge of an ocean. The silver arc of a bridge cut across water and sky, both at this hour filled with a progressively mellowing light. It was a favorite place for Angel and Rohit; they had often gone there and felt very close, sharing each other's thoughts. But now Rohit was telling his thoughts and Angel listened in silence, trying to hear the secret beneath the utterly candid and open, even somewhat naive demeanor he had always shown her; and detecting no shadow of it— when he was, as always, her friend, her brother, confiding in her completely—she said, "Won't you tell me about your brother."

He had been talking with enthusiasm about some language courses he was planning to take to help him advance in his job. Now he fell silent. He did not appear shocked, or even surprised: as though he had been expecting it, was always expecting it. He lowered his lashes over his eyes; a light was extinguished; after a while he said in a still voice, "Yes, Angel," admitting everything there was to admit.

She felt as though an unsuspected barrier had broken between them. At once a warm flow of affection seemed to go out of her heart into his—a very different feeling from the harsh and mostly painful tug there was between herself and Lara. He didn't ask how she had found out, accepting that sooner or later everyone did. They stayed on the bench by the parapet; the last glow of light finally faded out of water and sky, leaving them gray and drained but adorned by the bridge with the glitter of its own lights and those of the cars passing over it. Angel didn't really want him to tell her anything more; the silence between them seemed to her the deepest companionship they had ever had. At last they shared everything, and while this may not have been a relief to him, it was to her.

Later he told her a lot more, but that evening he spoke only about his mother. Angel already knew about their life in New Delhi; he had so often spoken of it and his childhood in the big modern house with the garden, rented for them by the company where his father was a top executive. The house was always full of guests, friends and relatives come to stay, and from early morning his mother was busy with plans for their entertainment. She drove them around on shopping trips in her own little car—his father had a company car with chauffeur—and in the evenings she gave dinner parties for them, serving pomfrets flown in fresh from Bombay and strawberries from Kashmir. She had had the same cook—Nathu Ram—for twenty-five years and had taught him every kind of sophisticated little dish. She was always learning different recipes, cutting out everything new that appeared in the women's weeklies and also enrolling in the cooking classes given privately by ladies skilled in continental cuisines. She had her regular day at the beauty salon, to be toned up by a body massage, along with facial and hairdo. She played a good game of golf at the club, and once a week she joined a group of friends at cards, followed by a lunch which they took turns giving one another.

It all came to an end. The father's firm was decent, they did not deprive him of his job or the house that went with it. But he could not stand it—the visits to the police court and to the jail, then to the criminal court for the trial, and the reporters outside with cameras waiting for the family. Before the three years of preliminaries and trial were over, the father had died of a cancer that had quickly devoured the body he had kept so healthy over the years with good food and games of tennis. But Mrs. Arora did not miss a single day in court or a single visit to the jail, where she made friends of the superintendent and the warders and the more influential inmates. When her husband died and they had to vacate the house, she moved herself and Rohit into two rooms in an area of moderate rents, at the opposite end of town from where her friends lived. This was just as well, for it was difficult keeping up relationships with them, however sympathetic they seemed to be; it was even embarrassing to meet Nathu Ram, her former cook, who had been snapped up by a neighboring family. Money ran low and she started her business of embroideries and fine linens, making use of the expert good taste she had acquired in her lavish housekeeping days. She did not hesitate to call on all her former friends and acquaintances to help her get established; by this time she had become very determined and there was no way she would let herself be gotten rid of, though some of them tried. Her strength grew and stood her in good stead once her son was sentenced: for now she was fighting for his life, in the appeals courts and in tireless pursuit of anyone who might be useful to her—lawyers, journalists, politicians, civil servants: she sat waiting on doorsteps, never letting herself be turned away and swallowing insults with a smile.

IT WAS ONE of those days when Angel knew, as soon as she entered the apartment, that Lara had been left alone in it too long. The air, churned around by the central air-conditioning plant, was exhausted, stale, and warmish. The windows were sealed tight, allowing nothing out and nothing in—not even the sounds of the city, which came as a faint drone behind the hum of the air-conditioning. The only indication of what it might be like outside was the unhealthy tinge of the sky, yellowed by the fumes from the city. Lara, unbathed, had obviously remained indoors the entire day, confined within these walls as well as within her own thoughts, which were as sealed in and self-generating as the air inside the apartment.

She had entirely convinced herself that the Aroras were criminals. By this time all her suspicions had become proofs, and Angel knew it was useless to try to contradict them. In any case, she was aware that what Lara really wanted was to be rescued from the misery caused by her own thoughts seething inside her. From the Aroras she went on to Helena, reviving the subject of the house—she said Helena had no right to live there, that it belonged to Hugo, too, and to the whole family, that is, to Angel and Lara herself. She tossed words around wildly: she said Helena was as bad as the Aroras, worse, for it was her own daughter and niece she was swindling—she taunted Angel with that word, *swindling,* your mother is a swindler, a cheat, she shouted it several times, daring Angel to contradict, to defend Helena, and Angel did not dare. When Lara shouted like that, she showed a gap in her perfect row of teeth, for the dentist had had to extract one that had become too rotten to be redeemed. It was in the lower jaw and showed only when she opened her mouth wide.

She was pacing the room—she looked wild with her unkempt tawny hair, and she was wearing a loose black caftan splashed all over with golden tigers leaping among bursts of sunflowers. The room was still empty of furniture; they had kept it that way as a space open to possibilities— principally the possibility of Lara taking up dancing again. Besides the telephone on the floor, the only purchase that had not been returned was the record player, along with a pile of discs chosen by Lara for the dance practice she was going to start any day. Hoping to change Lara's mood, Angel now had the good idea of putting on one of these discs. When the music, perfectly reproduced by the machine, suddenly and too loudly filled the room, she assumed a pleasant expression as if she liked it. But it was totally toneless and the jangled, frenzied sounds seemed to exacerbate Lara's nerves—she listened for a while, but then in a swift movement, her black caftan flapping around her, she strode toward the player, unplugged it, and flung it across the room in Angel's direction. It fell against the wall without hitting Angel, but the disc flew out and glanced against her cheek.

Angel's first thought was for the machine. She picked it up and carried it back to its original position. Of course it was broken and would never play again, but she fixed it in such a way that it appeared undamaged. That was all she was concerned about—that everything should appear normal, not only for when Peter came but for their own sakes too. The disc seemed all right, and she replaced it in its cover. All this while Lara stood stock-still in the middle of the room, her hands flung before her face so she would not have to see what had happened.

When Angel had finished tidying up, she went to the bathroom mirror to examine her cheek. It was bleeding from a cut made by the disc; she began to wash it with cotton and disinfectant, but every time she wiped the blood away, more came trickling out. Lara followed her—"Oh, no!" she cried at the sight of the blood, and again she flung up her hands to cover her eyes. Angel said, "It's not very deep."

"Let me see," said Lara. She held Angel's face, and Angel looked up at her trustingly. But almost at once Lara let go and turned away and made retching sounds. "It's horrible," she said.

"It really isn't," Angel assured her. "It's only that I can't stop the bleeding."

After a while Lara said: "I suppose you're going to run straight off to my father and tell him."

"Tell him what?"

"And you'll tell Peter too. You'll say that you don't want to stay here anymore."

Angel stopped swabbing her cheek and turned to put her arms around Lara's waist. She tried to press her close, but Lara made herself inert and passive. Angel just kept on standing there till she felt Lara relax; then she said, "I never will."

"All right," Lara said, believing her at once. "Let go of me, Angel, you're getting blood on me. What will you tell them? About this . . . this . . ." She indicated Angel's cut.

"Oh, this. I'll just say I hurt myself. With a can opener," she added at random. That made Lara laugh.

There was a sound at the front door, and Peter's voice called them as he let himself in with his key. Lara whispered, "Get a Band-Aid, quick." She scrabbled around for one in the bathroom cabinet and tried to put it on Angel's cheek herself, unsuccessfully—"You do it! I said be quick!" Peter called again from the room, she called back, "We're in here! That stupid Angel hurt herself!" When Peter appeared at the bathroom door, she said: "Look at her: isn't it the dumbest thing? She cut her cheek with a can opener—I *said* it was dumb—dumb, dumb Angel," and she kissed Angel, brushing her lips across her wounded cheek.

DURING THE FOLLOWING days Lara appeared to be quiet and contented. She told Angel she was working— "Writing," she said, and then she teased, "Oh, you think you're the only one who can write." She was busy the whole weekend, sitting cross-legged on the futon in her bedroom and covering sheets of yellow legal paper. She would not say what she was writing, only that she was "expressing her ideas." Angel was touched by the sight of her concentrating so hard; Lara paused to ponder while she gnawed at her ball-point and looked up at the ceiling with eyes as pure as a Madonna's.

Angel did not inquire what ideas she was expressing, but she found out a week later. While she was in the office, Helena called for her to come upstairs to the living room. Hugo was there too—it was like a family reunion in that familiar room where Angel had composed her first poems and Lara had performed her dance. The room was filled by late afternoon sunlight, and it lit up the flowers blooming on the upholstery Anna had chosen for her furniture. It also lit up the yellow legal papers with Lara's writing on them, which lay scattered between Helena and Hugo.

Helena reached out a page to Angel, who took it reluctantly. She didn't have to do more than run her eyes over it. Helena silently handed her another page and another, and Angel silently took them. Each page was the same. Some lines were very fluid and not a word crossed out, and others were scratched over so vigorously that the paper had holes in it. Most sentences were childish and illiterate in expression—"You are a selfish old bitch and must be stoped"—but then suddenly they became quite sophisticated: "You are sick inside with neurotic posessivness . . . You are compulsivly unable to releise any object or person in your grasp . . ." Only the spelling was uniformly awful.

Angel did not give the pages back but held on to them, hoping they could be hers and no one else need ever see them. But meanwhile Helena and Hugo *had* seen them, and Angel got herself ready to put up a defense. To her relief, it turned out that they blamed her more than they did Lara—for living shut up alone with her—and she so quickly and gladly admitted that it was her fault that Helena was surprised into reversing herself: "Why, what did you do?"

"It's more what I didn't do," Angel eagerly tried to explain. She thought this was true and promised herself there and then that in the future she would take better care.

Hugo guessed her thoughts: "She needs more than you can do for her," he said. "But what you could do is try to persuade her to see someone, and I have several possibilities of people who might be right for her."

Angel didn't want to contradict him—who was a doctor as well as her father—but she rejected his position utterly. She felt strengthened in her conviction that she herself knew best by being in this room with Anna and Siegfried looking out as benignly from their photograph as they had done throughout all the years of her childhood side by side on their couch, radiating love and uncritical approval. It was Angel's ambition to create a similar climate for Lara in which she would be able to unfold and blossom.

Hugo said, "You have to have someone else help her—help us all to help her."

"A stranger," Angel said.

"A qualified stranger, Angel. A doctor."

"Lara is not sick."

In the ensuing silence Angel was intensely aware of the incriminating papers she was holding. When she spoke again, it was defensively: "Lara has medication. I told you and you said it was all right—"

"It might no longer be enough. That's why I want her to go to someone, even if it's no more than to correct her prescription—"

"You're a doctor," Angel interrupted. "You can do that. Why don't you?" She decided to make some concession: "She *is* excitable, I'm not saying she's not. She goes higher than other people—like someone taking a higher note in singing? That happens to be the way she is. But if you'd tell me something I could give her, she'd be all right." She stared at him stubbornly through her glasses. He shrugged, threw up his hands—Hugo was characteristically quick to capitulate, and Angel quickly followed up and said she would come by his house to get the prescription.

But Helena had not finished yet: "And meanwhile, what about you? And your work?"

"I come to the office every day."

Helena brushed aside this flippant reply. She indicated her parents: "How disappointed they'd have been." Angel had gotten up, still holding the papers in her hand. Helena went on: "They used to sit here and have these long talks about how their granddaughter was going to be a famous poet." Then she said: "I'm afraid all the time. I can't sleep at night, I'm so afraid."

Her words seemed to find an echo in Hugo, for he took her up very quickly. "She won't do anything to herself—she's too timid for that, too dependent."

"Yes, on me," Angel said eagerly. "She depends on me and I will see her through."

"It's for *you* I'm afraid!" Helena cried. "What she will do to you."

"Oh, no," Hugo said, again too quickly. "She would be very careful not to hurt Angel."

"Hasn't she hurt her already?"

Helena may have meant this in a more general sense, but Angel's hand flew to her cheek: "I told you—I cut myself!"

"You told me that you cut yourself on a can opener," Helena said dryly, "and I still haven't worked it out how anyone can do that."

Angel laughed: "Yes, it was really stupid; really dumb."

"Why don't *you* ask her, Hugo, what really happened. Perhaps she'll tell *you* the truth."

Seeing Hugo hesitate—perhaps afraid to ask—Angel took quick advantage: "But it *is* the truth, why do you have to be so suspicious." She, too, addressed Hugo: "I don't know what's come over Mother—she misinterprets everything and is so hostile to Lara and me."

"Oh, yes, *I'm* hostile," Helena said, indicating the legal papers, which made Angel hold them closer to herself, defending her possession of them. So then Helena turned to her brother and spoke to him bitterly: "You're concerned only about your own daughter. You don't care for Angel and me—if you did, wouldn't you say something to help me, help me! Oh, I'm not asking Angel to come back to me, there she must do what she wishes, but to get out of the situation she's in with your daughter—" Then she saw his face as he stood there white and speechless, and she stepped up close to him and hid her face against his shoulder and he put his arm around her. Well, thought Angel, let them have it out with each other—and while they were thus engaged, she stole out with Lara's letter.

She ran up to her own bedroom. She quickly threw the pages into the grate of the fireplace, where she had always burned her discarded poems. She found matches in her desk, and along with them some pages of her old manuscripts—poems she had written and thrust away in the drawer. She took them out, and without bothering to glance at them she tossed them in the grate together with Lara's pages. She lit a match and watched them all go up in flames. Her back was to the window, so she didn't notice that the sky behind the high-rise buildings was also in flames, from the evening sun dissolving in it. She continued to watch the fire in the grate licking at Lara's yellow pages and her own white ones, rising higher and consuming them, then dying down till there was only a little heap of black ash.

. . .

ANGEL TOOK HUGO at his word and went to see him to get a prescription. She was met by one of his girl-friends—they were known collectively as the Valkyries, but this particular one was called Helgabeth. She told Angel that Hugo was working in his study and was on no account to be disturbed. Helgabeth herself had come to deliver a Georgian coffeepot that Hugo had bought and forgotten to collect; she had been about to leave but now was glad of the opportunity to chat for a while with Angel and get to know her better. But it was she who did all the talking—about Hugo and his work: she loved speaking on this subject and did so with a kind of exultation. Like all Hugo's girlfriends, she was blond and married, with a superbly developed bosom that may have given or, anyway, was capable of giving milk. She had been a photographer's model, and even when expounding the more abstruse points of Hugo's work, she kept her professional poise, one superb leg crossed over the other, her skirt hitched over her knee. She spoke fluent English but with a Scandinavian intonation, which gave what she said an echo as of other realms, supernal and strange.

Hugo's work—as interpreted by Helgabeth—was nothing less than fashioning a new humanity. For this he made use of various disciplines, which he carried far beyond their own limits. Psychoanalysis, for one, could go so far and no further. It was useful in clearing the ground and cutting through the tangled weeds of wrongly sown emotions; but once that preliminary task was done, the more important digging could begin, and for this other methods were used, both very new and very old—some as old as the human race, said Helgabeth with a lift of her head. All conceptions and preconceptions had to be left entirely behind, the mind itself, conventional human thought, broken out of its habitual mode. Here Zen koans were useful implements, as well as dreams. Dreams! said Helgabeth; she had had some extraordinary ones, revealing depths of her psyche that reached beyond human history into archaeology, even geology. Yet the journey did not end there, for it was still within the range of the natural universe; whereas what had to be reached was—here she smiled mysteriously and said, no, she was not using any word denoting anything beyond natural: instead, following Hugo, she was leaving a blank there.

"A blank," Angel repeated, and she must have sounded disappointed, for Helgabeth went on to reassure her. There were schools of thought that deliberately drew back from expressing the inexpressible—not, she protested, that Hugo and his followers allied themselves with mystics of any kind; on the contrary, they drew a sharp line between themselves and these often pathetic individuals, many of them complete neurotics, or epileptics, or foolish to the point of idiocy. Whereas Hugo would not allow anyone into his classes who did not possess absolute physical and mental health, for the first requisite in transcending one's own faculties was to be in complete command of them. The work was too hard for invalids.

HELGABETH WAS A shining example of absolute health, but Hugo himself fell well below his own standards. This struck Angel when next day she unexpectedly saw him waiting for her in the lobby of her apartment building.

His face sagged with anxiety, and his thinning hair stood on end as though he had been running his hands through it. He nearly missed Angel, for there were many people walking past the doormen and the security desk. Hugo himself had not been able to pass, he informed her wryly: he had had himself announced, but Lara had refused to let him up. Now he rode the elevator with Angel; he said, "I guess she doesn't want to see me because of the letter." Angel would have liked to say, "What letter?" but realized that not everyone was as prepared as she was to pretend it had not been written.

For someone who had just refused to grant him permission to enter, Lara appeared pleased to see her father. She at once took up her teasing, mock-exasperated manner with him—straightened his collar, said he needed a haircut, and why weren't the Valkyries looking after him properly? When he asked why she had told the doormen not to let him up, she said, "Oh, was that you? I thought it was some boring old man I didn't want to see." She stuck the tip of her tongue out, smiling to herself about him.

Angel apologized for the lack of furniture—there wasn't even a chair he could sit on: "It's really Lara's studio," she said. "For her dance practice." At this, still in a teasing mood with him, Lara executed a few dance steps that took her clear across the room where, making a curtsy and spreading her arms, she ended up in a cross-legged position on the floor. The room seemed to vibrate from her rapid movements, which had all the force of her healthy young body behind them, though not a dancer's grace.

Hugo said, "You've started writing letters again." He was still standing with his raincoat over his arm, as though about to leave. But he wasn't; he, too, got down on the floor next to her. "I thought you weren't going to do that anymore."

"I'll do it if I have to."

"Why do you have to?"

"Because it's my house."

They were together in the intimacy of two people with a long and secret history between them. For a moment Angel felt excluded, but he glanced up at her and then back at Lara: "If it's your house, it's Angel's, too, and she's not writing any letters."

"Yes, she wrote it with me. She helped me." Lara continued her teasing tone with him, winking at Angel to show how they were together, united against Hugo.

He said, "She didn't help you write the letters to your mother."

"Angel didn't *know* Mother," said Lara, patiently reasonable with him.

"If she had, do you think she would have written to her the way you did?"

Still Lara did not blink; her eyes remained wide open, fixed on her father in utter frankness. "I never wrote to Mother."

"And you didn't write to Helena either?"

Lara laughed at him: "I'm not listening!" She put her hands over her ears. Hugo remained beside her; for someone so loose-limbed, he appeared at that moment remarkably stable and rooted.

Lara stopped laughing. Gloom overcame her. She uncovered the ears she had so playfully stopped. She said, "It was you who said Mother was crazy and sent her to that place."

"No, I didn't. I wasn't there. I was in Santa Barbara. I came only when they sent for me, and by then they had found your letters."

"I wrote her nice letters." As swiftly and skillfully as she had sunk down, Lara leaped up; her wide skirt swishing, she was in her bedroom in a flash and could be heard to lock the door.

"Let her come home with me," Hugo said to Angel. "It's better while she's in this mood." With an effort he added: "I don't want things to get any worse for you."

It also cost Angel an effort to say, "It'd be worse for me if I wasn't with her. . . . Not knowing what was happening to her." Making an even greater effort, she admitted, "And just not being with her."

Both listened for sounds from the bedroom; but there were none. "She'll turn against you," Hugo said. "Like she's done against me."

"She's very fond of you."

"Yes. Sometimes."

Angel was disinclined to continue talking about Lara with Hugo. She was ready to admit that he meant almost as well by Lara as she herself did, but it was not possible to pretend that the situation was other than that she and Lara were on one side and everyone else, including Lara's father (and her own), on another.

Also, she had some practical business with Hugo. She went to the bathroom to get Lara's pills. He scrutinized the labels, then wrote out a new prescription and carefully instructed Angel—she listened as carefully—exactly what to give when. While they were doing this, Lara appeared in the door. She held an unlit cigarette in one hand and the other she laid on her hip in an attitude of defiance. But she looked miserable more than defiant.

Angel told her what they were doing and Hugo also explained about the change in medication he was trying out for her. She interrupted him: "Doesn't anyone have a match?" They began to hunt around—Hugo said he no longer carried matches since the time he had stopped smoking; finally Angel found some in the kitchen and helped Lara light her cigarette. Lara inhaled inexpertly— she hardly ever smoked, only using it quite literally as a smoke screen when something unpleasant was going on. But their search for a match had drawn them closer, and all three went and sat together on the bed in Angel's room, like people ready to discuss and work together.

Angel said the trouble was that she had to leave Lara alone so much. They debated the alternatives. Lara could move back in with Hugo; or Angel and she could move to Helena's house; or Angel could give up her job with Helena. Lara said she would agree to whatever they decided. She was sad and humble, and both of them were eager to do whatever was best for her, regardless of themselves. Angel felt tremendously relieved, for it seemed to her that with so much love and goodwill, everything must turn out well.

Then Lara said in a small voice, "No wonder you all wish I was dead." She gave Angel her cigarette and asked her to put it out, please; and to Hugo she said, "You wanted it for Mother and now you want it for me." She raised her voice: "Mother always said you'd be perfectly happy if it wasn't for her and me! That's why she kept on trying: so you could be perfectly happy." She turned to Angel: "Then he made out it was because of me she did it, because I wrote letters to her. Of course I wrote letters to her! She treated me so badly."

Her eyes roved around their faces and around the room —she appeared hunted, and also as though hunting for someone to blame. Hugo put out his hand and laid it on the back of her neck to draw her close to himself; and although she said to Angel, "Don't let him touch me," he persisted in pressing her face against himself, tacitly admitting that after being a doctor, a psychiatrist, and a philosopher, it was all he could think to do for her.

MRS. ARORA TOLD Helena that certain days carried a malign influence, and she insisted on performing the same mitigating ceremonies in Helena's house as she did in her own. She walked up and down the stairs with a lace handkerchief on her head, carrying a bowl with incense smoking in it and chanting some formulae in a long-dead language unknown even to herself. The mysterious sounds, as well as the smell and smoke of the incense, filled the house and made it strange. Mrs. Arora always fasted on those days. Helena failed to take any of it seriously, but Mrs. Arora didn't mind as long as she was permitted to ward off whatever threatening influences there were hovering around.

Respecting Mrs. Arora's wish to keep her new friendship separate from her past, Angel never spoke to Helena about the Aroras' secret. But she and Rohit often spoke of it: now that she knew, it seemed to be a tremendous relief to him to be able to talk to her. He would come to the office and wait for her to finish, accepting that the only time she had available nowadays was on her way between the house and where Lara was waiting for her. Inside the house he never said a word about his brother; it was as though he feared to leave one trace of a thought in this new place where his mother had established herself. But once out in the street he was ready to say anything—perhaps half hoping that the rush and roar of the traffic would carry his words away, like someone shouting out his feelings against wind and waves.

As time passed, Angel received a strong impression of his dead brother's personality. Vikram, seven years older than Rohit, had always had something irresistible about him, especially to his mother. When he was small she had been enchanted by his ability to overcome her resistance to anything he wanted, whether it was to make a tent out of her best saris or to go to the circus every day. When she tried to say no, he wheedled her till she gave in; then she laughed and proudly told everyone how clever he was at twisting her around his little finger. But when Vikram grew older, he no longer wheedled, he demanded—and now it was no longer for things she could give him but for money to buy pleasures he didn't tell her about. He was often desperate for money, and there were violent scenes between them. Once, when he wanted her to sell her jewelry and she refused, he tore at the gold earrings in her pierced lobes—Rohit, cowering in his room, heard her shriek of pain. Some years later, in prison, Vikram noticed that she was no longer wearing those earrings. When she told him that she had had to sell them to pay for his defense, he got in a rage—he said that if she had sold them at the time he had asked her to, he would not have been forced into doing what he had done.

It was a winter evening when Rohit told Angel about this last incident, and by the time they got to where Angel lived with Lara, it was already dark. A new superstructure was coming up opposite, and its skeleton reared up enormously into the cold sky. Angel had long ago stopped asking Rohit to come up with her to see Lara; in fact, they no longer mentioned Lara. As usual, they said good-bye at some distance from the entrance, and then Rohit turned away in one direction and Angel in the other. On that winter evening she hesitated before she entered, and a little shudder passed over her. It had happened once or twice before, but this time it was due to what Rohit had been telling her about his brother.

LARA WAS DOCILE about taking the new pills Hugo had prescribed, but they made her sleep a great deal. She could sleep right through a day and a night, getting up only to go to the bathroom or sit dully at a meal that Angel had prepared for her. It was around this time that Angel stopped being vegetarian, for she often had to eat up the steaks and hamburgers she had cooked—they were Lara's favorite food, but she was too sleepy to eat them. While she slept, Angel sat beside her and made plans for both of them. She thought of the money she was saving to enable them to go away anytime they wanted, anyplace in the world. Only she never could think of anywhere they could go and be free of what disturbed them here. Sometimes she made up such a place: it was a garden that had marble paths inlaid with what looked like gems and a fountain and many evergreen trees. Here she and Lara walked hand in hand, and there wasn't another soul around and no sound except of birds and the water springing up from the fountain and falling back again in a spray of crystal drops.

Even on the days when Lara was not asleep they stayed mostly in her bedroom. Angel bought a nest of little tables and some collapsible chairs, and they entertained their visitors in there too—that is, Peter, and the receptionists from downstairs, and Roland; now and again there were acquaintances Lara had made in her wanderings around the streets, such as people working in neighboring stores whom she invited up for a drink.

One day when Angel returned from the office, Roland was there, wearing nothing but his underpants. He was embarrassed and at once began to put on his shirt; but Lara was amused, she said, "We've shocked Angel." Angel may have had a shock, but she was not shocked, having long ago taught herself that it was natural for intimate friends to be intimate together; and certainly, compared with other people who came up, Roland *was* an intimate friend, or at least someone they had known for some time.

Another day she found him clearing up in the bedroom, where a party appeared to have taken place. The tables were scattered around with dirty glasses on them and filled ashtrays. Angel tried to help him, but he was more effective than she was, trained by his waiter's job. He told her about Lara's visitors. They were three building contractors from upstate New York who had come into the city for the day, on business and, if possible, some entertainment. Lara had found them marooned on the benches set on the island between two roaring torrents of traffic going up and down Broadway. They were middle-aged, awkward, and shy, but when Lara invited them home, they were prepared to dare one another on to be bold. However, by the time Roland had arrived—visiting on his afternoon off—they were sitting stiffly on the collapsible chairs, staring straight in front of them. Lara, cross-legged on her futon, was describing something called the phoenix dance, occasionally waving her arms about. They were all drinking wine, the three men grasping the stems of their glasses in their big fists. Roland walked around in a disapproving way, opening windows to shoo out the smoke from the visitors' cigarettes. They shamefacedly stubbed them out but remained rooted on their chairs. It wasn't that they were spellbound by what she was saying—Roland guessed that all they knew about dance was what they had done years before at their high school proms with their then girlfriends, now their wives. But they were rigid with the social embarrassment of people in a situation where they did not know how to behave; and worse, there was the fear of being trapped in the bedroom of a girl who was so weird that she was probably sick in her head.

Fortunately, one of the lobby receptionists had come up —for a chat (and who knew what else, Roland grimly commented) before going off duty. Between them, he and Roland had managed to divert Lara and ease the three men out of their chairs and the apartment, giving them directions to Grand Central for their trains back home. But Roland warned Angel about the situation: Lara alone all day up here, bored and ready for any company—building employees, store clerks, or just people off the streets; she would be better off in the hotel, or anyplace else where someone could keep an eye on her.

THE ARORAS' LEASE on their tiny apartment was expiring, and Helena had a new idea. She wanted to move Rohit and Mrs. Arora into the house with her—they spent so much time with her anyway, they might as well live there. But of course first Helena consulted Angel and came down to the office for that purpose. It was one of the frequent moments when Angel was not quite concentrating on her work but was brooding about what Lara might be doing. When Helena spoke of her plan, Angel was startled because she had just been thinking how much easier it would be for her if she could move Lara into the house and keep an eye on her all day. Helena, who had mentioned her idea tentatively, testing out Angel's reaction to it, said, "Of course I won't if you don't want me to."

"It's not that," Angel replied. When she could not say what it was, not being ready yet with her own plan, Helena continued: "I feel the same about the house as you do— that I want to keep it just as it was."

"It isn't just as it was."

"You're right, it isn't—your grandparents aren't actually here anymore but I want it to be as if they were. And also, if they'd walk back in tomorrow, they should feel at once that it was home, their home. . . . And, of course, you, too, darling, if you were to come back."

This last she said timidly, lest it should in any way be interpreted either as a demand or a reproach; but also tenderly to make it known that it was a possibility forever open. While she spoke, and for some time after, she stroked Angel's cheek and her hair; and this loving gesture filled Angel with gratitude but also some pain, for she was no longer accustomed to such tenderness.

Usually, when her office hours were over, she did not go into the house but straight from the basement into the street, to get home as fast as possible. Today, thinking over what Helena had said, she went up the main staircase, first into the living room, where it was true Siegfried and Anna could at any moment have entered and found themselves back home with nothing changed. Angel tried to think how it would be if the Aroras moved in, with Mrs. Arora sprinkling rosewater and blessings all over the house, and it seemed to her that although theirs would be a very different presence, it would not be a disturbing one. No, she thought, she would not mind Rohit and his mother moving in, might even like it—provided she did not need the place for Lara. It was when she thought of Lara being there that Angel's instincts rose as though in defense of her childhood home. But of course, and all the same, Lara had first claim.

Angel went up two more flights to what had been her own room. Unlike all the others, this room seemed truly vacant, although here, too, as in the rest of the house, the furniture was still in place. Some of her clothes remained hanging in her closet, looking like things waiting to be disposed of. She sat down in her chair by the window. The last bluish tinge in the sky was already eclipsed by the lights coming on in the buildings; high up on the top of some of them commercial signs shimmered brilliantly. For the first time since very long ago, Angel thought of the poetry she had tried to write there, and found that she could not even remember, except in the vaguest way, what it had been about. She opened the drawer of her table, but there were only some spent ball-points, a used stamp, matches, and paper clips; the pages of her poetry had of course been burned by herself. What was it she had tried to say? Her subject had always been elusive—always beyond her reach —at least after those rapturous years of earliest youth when it had been easy to write about birds, clouds, and flowers, and from there a natural step to love and other sweet emotions. But her later subject—or object of desire—had become more difficult, having nothing to do with what went on around her or the feelings attached to that, but with something surmised in the dying light and in the towering buildings reaching as high as they could and yet never high enough: beyond the people she loved, beyond the city, beyond anything she could grasp with her mind or senses and yet more intimate and resonant than anything else known to or felt by her. It was for that she had sought and never yet found the words and now never would because of having given up looking for them.

PETER SAID, "WHEN did you last see your grandmother?"

"Not so long ago."

"How did you find her?"

"Same as usual," Angel said vaguely, then added, "Fine."

Peter did not contradict, but there was a cool look in his eyes that meant he had a different opinion and would act on it. Angel became uneasy, for the truth was that lately her communication with Grandmother Koenig and Rose had been entirely by telephone. She kept meaning to go and see them—she promised them she would—but once back from the office she found it difficult to leave Lara again. She persuaded herself that they were doing well— Rose said they were, though with a little hesitation which it was easy to ignore, for it was not in Rose's nature to speak with confidence. As for Grandmother Koenig, she had stopped complaining about Rose; in fact, she never mentioned her, instead she spoke of someone called Tetta whom Angel could not identify. One day she said that she and Tetta had been to Rumpelmayer's for hot chocolate, another time that they had gone shopping for a coat at Altman's; all that sounded pleasant enough and Angel thought of herself as reassured.

But the morning after Peter's questioning, there was a panicky call from Rose: "Mr. Koenig was here and it was one of her bad days." Angel left the office and hurried over to see them. The elevator man took her up to Grandmother Koenig's floor, but there Angel had to wait outside the door while Rose fumbled with all the locks and chains inside to let her in. Rose whispered that she had to double-lock everything for fear of Grandmother Koenig getting out again.

Grandmother Koenig was ensconced in her usual place

in the drawing room, but now in front of the TV set, rolled in from the kitchen, where it had always been. She appeared to be watching a game show with pleasure, but when Rose turned it off she kept her face turned on the empty screen with the same pleasure. She was wearing a cotton housedress and a cardigan put on back to front. Rose explained that she had given up dressing her in her former stately attire: it took so long and was a struggle for both of them, and hardly was it over when Grandmother Koenig tried to take it all off again. And they didn't do all that with her hair anymore either—Rose stroked it while Grandmother Koenig smiled—it took so much time, and it was really much more natural just combed and pinned. But if Mr. Koenig had given them some warning that he was coming, Rose could easily have got Grandmother Koenig into one of her crepe dresses and girdle and stockings, and also she would have had time to clean up a bit in here, do some dusting and vacuuming and roll the TV back into the kitchen.

The room was even darker than usual, for more bulbs had gone out in the chandeliers and had not been replaced. But it was a cozy darkness, and for the first time since Angel had known it, the room looked lived-in: lived in by Rose, that is, with her cigarette butts crushed in more than one ashtray as well as in a saucer of spilled coffee. Grandmother Koenig at once began to tell Angel how she had gone to the park and thrown bread crumbs to the ducks. After a while Angel realized that this had taken place not yesterday nor the day before, but some seventy-five years before and in the company of someone called Tetta, who had scolded Grandmother Koenig for getting mud on her white socks.

"She calls me Tetta a lot of the time," smiled Rose. "And that's why she's been trying to get out—she thinks it's time for her walk with Tetta or to go for coffee and cake with her aunt Minna or someone." When the doormen found her downstairs in her housedress and slippers, they were very obsequious and nice with her, even when she got on her high horse and said she would have them dismissed for not letting her out. They alerted Rose, and by the time she got down, Grandmother Koenig was quite willing to accompany her back upstairs, though very indignant with the doormen, and Rose had to promise to complain about them to Peter. Afterward, when Grandmother Koenig was in bed, Rose hurried down to tip them. They were very understanding. They were all old men who had been in this old building for a long time and had held the door open for ladies who, once regal in furs and long dresses, had in the course of the years turned into confused and bedraggled old women.

Peter's unexpected arrival, Rose said, had upset Grand-mother Koenig in a bad way, undoing days of calm and quiet, when she hadn't once tried to run away or take her clothes off or do anything else she shouldn't. But as soon as Peter had come in, she had done just that, and quick as a flash too, while Rose was busy emptying out some ashtrays. The next thing Rose knew, there was this commotion by the front door with Grandmother Koenig stark naked try-ing to get out and Peter to stop her. Rose had soon had a robe over her and put her back in the drawing room and into her frock: it had happened before and wasn't such a very big deal. Old people did get a bit eccentric now and then, and no wonder considering all they had been through: Rose often wondered about herself, how she had managed to keep herself together with all that had happened in her life which was hardly half as long as Grandmother Koenig's. And anyway, what was so terrible about wanting to take your clothes off—you had to understand the psychology behind it, and wouldn't anyone want to do the same if all their life long they had had to be dressed up in all those clothes and underclothes, no matter what?

"I can look after her very easily on my own, really I can," urged Rose. "See the way I put her little jacket on her back to front, she can't take anything off now even if she wanted to, which most of the time she doesn't. She's all right, she's very well, she's happy—we both are, if they'll only leave us alone," pleaded Rose. The contentment that had begun to bloom on her face was already fading back into the strained, pinched expression that was more natural to her.

IT WAS ONLY a few days later that alerted by Rose's anguished call, Angel hurried again to Grandmother Koenig's. There she found Peter's wife, Lilian, making an inventory of everything in the apartment. She had enlisted Rose as her assistant and had made her take out all the dinner and dessert services stacked away in sideboards and pantry. Lilian was very brisk and efficient. It was amazing how little she had changed over the years. Her figure was still as small, neat, and compact as when Peter had first seen her in her white coat as his dentist's assistant, and she still wore her hair swept up in the style becoming to her tiny features.

Notepad and pencil in hand, she was walking between the rows of china laid out on the carpets. Curtains and shutters had been opened to let in as much natural light as possible; but, owing to the adjacent buildings, this was not enough, and Rose had been made to climb on a stepladder to replace the dead bulbs in the chandeliers. She was in tears.

Lilian led Angel into the dining room, where the table had been pulled out to its full extent, as for one of the great dinner parties of the past. It was stacked from end to end with champagne, wine, liqueur, and every other kind of glasses and decanters. Sliding the doors shut against Rose— "Where's your grandmother's diamond bracelet?" Lilian demanded. "And her gold fob-watch?"

"They must be in the bank with the rest of her jewelry."

"They're not, Angel." Lilian looked grim. They were both standing, for all the chairs were loaded with silverware and fine table linens. "She always kept them to wear here, didn't you know that? And now they're gone."

Angel, very much aware of Rose on the other side of the door, and maybe with her ear against it, said, "Rose has been wonderful. I don't know what we'd do without her."

Lilian continued to look grim: "We'll do without her very soon—well, of course! Your grandmother needs professional care."

"Oh, no—they're happy—"

"They?"

"She and Rose."

Lilian gave an incredulous laugh, then piled a set of Rosenthal side plates onto their matching dinner plates, making an angry clatter. "Don't let your father hear you say that, because that wasn't his impression when he came here the other day. Peter was furious. *Furious,"* she repeated, sounding it herself. "He told me to get in here at once and start packing up—he was mad at *me* as though it were *my* fault. Not that I'm not used to your father blaming me for whatever goes wrong. I'm supposed to make everything perfect for him, that's what I'm there for." She spoke bitterly but also with satisfaction. What she said was undeniable, Angel knew from her own experience. Whenever Angel had been sent as a child to spend time with her father, it had been left to Lilian to make her stay agreeable; she had tried her best, and though failing every time, had never shirked trying again.

She was kneeling on the carpet, opening velvet-lined cases of antique silverware which, though unused for decades, had retained all its sparkle. When Lilian looked up, this sparkle seemed to have been absorbed by her eyes— they glittered with that greed of which Grandmother Koenig had always accused her second daughter-in-law. She took out a fork and, examining its hallmark, "I thought so," she said with deep pleasure, and then without pleasure but very correctly, she added, "Peter says you must take anything you want, Angel."

"What would I do with it."

"Don't be silly. You'll get married one of these days—"

Lilian trailed off, maybe for lack of conviction, but

more likely because the doors were slowly sliding open. Rose's head appeared between them, mournfully surveying the scene of dissolution. In recognition of where authority now lay, she asked Lilian what to do next—but Lilian had already scrambled to her feet and slid the doors shut again so fast that Rose hardly had time to withdraw her head. However, in that brief moment she had managed to throw a look of reproach at Angel, which lingered behind.

"I'm going to fire her the moment I've settled your grandmother," Lilian said. She stepped up closer to whisper: "We've got to do something about the jewelry before she walks off with any more of it."

She led the way to Grandmother Koenig's bedroom. The inventory had not yet reached here, and everything was as usual. Grandmother Koenig had been kept in bed, propped up in a champagne-colored bedjacket and with a fresh rose of the same color in a vase beside her. Her hands were folded serenely over the coverlet. She appeared gratified to see Angel and let herself be kissed; nor did she bat an eyelid when Lilian also bent down to kiss her.

Lilian went over to the dressing table and took out the ivory-inlaid box containing the pieces of jewelry Grandmother Koenig kept at home. To get a better light, Lilian opened the curtains that had kept the bedroom shrouded in a rose-colored dusk. Grandmother Koenig turned her face toward the window and toward Lilian poring over her jewelry, but still her calm and amiable expression did not change.

"I've looked everywhere," said Lilian, scrabbling through the box, "and they're just not here. No, they're not in the vault either, because I've checked. Take what you want, Angel, and I'll have to carry the rest home with me."

"Lilian, you know I don't wear that kind of thing."

"Peter wants you to have it. He said Angel has to take what she wants first. . . . Look at this: how pretty." She ran a gold chain longingly through her fingers. She didn't lower her voice or turn around to see if there was any reaction from Grandmother Koenig; anyway, there wasn't. "Only you, Angel: he didn't say anything about your mother. Of course, she's not a Koenig and neither is your cousin." She lifted her chin, proud and firm with only the tiniest sag under it. "Whatever his faults," she said, "basically your father is a serious person; and certainly when it's a question of something serious like his mother's jewelry. He's not going to give it away, to your cousin or anyone else."

There was the smallest rattle at the door, and when Angel turned her head, she saw that the handle was moving. It was Rose asking to be let in, though hopelessly.

"I'm going to search her room," Lilian said. "She's not going to get away with anything. No one is. It's yours—and mine, to keep for when the boys get married. Now, take what you want quickly, Angel, so I can put it away."

"I'll take that," Angel said, and she extended her hand for the chain Lilian had been admiring.

"Really? Are you sure? . . . Well, all right." Lilian quickly shut the box and slid it into the big leather tote she had brought with her.

Angel thrust the chain into the pocket of her skirt. She turned around to Grandmother Koenig, who still lay calm and peaceful with her face toward the window. Angel realized that she had never quite noted the color of her grandmother's eyes. Perhaps because she had always seen her in her dark drawing room, she had had some vague idea that they were brown; now, by natural light, she saw that they were china blue. But they were so faded that they appeared colorless—as translucent as glass to the light of heaven streaming through the windowpanes.

LARA LIKED GRANDMOTHER Koenig's gold chain very much; she put it on at once and kept it on even when she went to bed. Angel saw her lying asleep with her fingers curled around it. She had kicked off her bedclothes and Angel put them back. She had gotten into the habit of checking up on Lara at night, waking with a start because she thought or dreamed that something untoward was happening. But nowadays she always found her asleep—as was to be expected, since she had herself seen to it that Lara took her tranquilizers. In fact, lately she had increased the dose though intending to cut it down again as soon as Lara was over her spell of restlessness.

The next day, when Angel came home, Lara was still wearing the chain. It was the only thing she was wearing. She appeared from the bedroom and laughingly called back into it: "It's only Angel!" Naked, she brushed past her, saying, "I'm dying of thirst," and could be heard humming to herself in the kitchen, where she poked around in the refrigerator.

When the young man emerged from the bedroom—it was one of the receptionists from downstairs—he was struggling into the black jacket he wore as a uniform and had not yet zippered his pants. Angel did her best to greet him normally; this made him more shamefaced, and his lips formed to make some excuse for his presence, but finding none, he glided out and shut the front door as gently as possible in an attempt to erase his presence. When she reappeared from the kitchen, Lara was drinking from a carton of milk—"Has he gone?" she asked and, amused at Angel: "Your *face.*"

Angel did not know what her face was registering at that moment. It may have been shock, but there was another, stronger emotion that made her avert her eyes from her cousin. Lara was tall, with rounded hips and breasts and full thighs, her legs tapering off to slender ankles; her nakedness was set off by the gold around her neck. She was drinking milk straight from the carton, which enhanced her aura of health and vitality. It was only her face that marred this total impression—not that it was not lovely, but that it was not quite aligned; though the features were perfectly regular, it was as if something were somewhere askew—was there an almost imperceptible tic, or a squint in her swimming deep eyes? If there was, Angel did not want to notice it.

Lara began defending herself: "What else can I do? I'm bored out of my mind all day, and he wanted to come up. And I like him; he's nice; he's got a terrific physique— don't you think? Angel? Oh, but you wouldn't know about anything like that, would you." Again she laughed at Angel and took a swig of milk.

Angel had never felt desire for anyone except Lara. It

was a completely alien sensation for her, and one that filled her with shame about herself. Yet she knew that what was for her the utter purity of Lara's beautiful body was frequently touched by other hands: Peter, Roland, the receptionist—anyone could come and make free with what Angel felt herself too unworthy to approach even in her thoughts.

"I like him better than Roland," Lara said. "Roland's a jerk—reading books about Tibet and seeing all these foreign movies—I mean he's just a waiter, isn't he, in a hotel." Suddenly she said, "You're the only person I really like."

Angel, much shorter than Lara, had her eyes level with her cousin's lips, which were at that moment dripping milk. Lara bent down and lightly brushed those lips—soft, rosy, moist, and milky—against Angel's. Angel looked straight into Lara's eyes—there may have been a squint, or perhaps nothing more than a shadow, but whatever it was, it was temporary and very likely due to the pills Angel was going to stop giving her as soon as she was better.

LILIAN HAD MADE a thorough job of the apartment. The massive pieces of furniture remained in place, but everything movable—clocks, carpets, silver, vases, pictures—had been safely stored away. Peter's footsteps echoed on the bare parquet flooring as he walked from room to room, surveying the apartment. He appeared satisfied on all counts, including his mother, who was back in her usual place in the drawing room, wearing a smock as simple as that of the professional nurse who had been engaged in place of Rose. Grandmother Koenig's hair had been shorn into a snow-white bob, very easy to keep tidy. The nurse kept running a comb through it and patting it down, while her eyes followed Peter on his inspection tour.

Angel, who had been summoned by Peter, walked behind him. He even went into what had been Rose's room, now completely emptied of her presence. In place of her bottle of Scotch and blue-eyed Jesus, there was a jar of cold cream probably belonging to the night nurse. When Angel asked him about Rose, Peter looked grim: "She was glad to beat it out of here before the police got on to her." Angel's reaction irritated him more: "I suppose *you* think it's all right for her to walk off with Mother's diamond bracelet and gold watch."

"How do you know she took them?" Angel said. "You don't know."

He was not prepared either to argue with or to let her into his plans. Instead, he said: "I had a canceled lunch today, so I went around to your place."

"Oh, yes?" Angel said in a very steady voice. "Was Lara home?"

"At first I thought she wasn't. I rang, I called, and in the end I let myself in."

Angel felt trapped with him there in the little room, and also afraid of what she might hear. She walked away from him, through the kitchen, the bare dining room, the drawing room where Grandmother Koenig and her nurse sat, holding hands like the best of friends. Angel kissed her grandmother's shorn head and was about to sit with them when Peter followed and indicated that he had to speak to

her alone. They went into Grandmother Koenig's bedroom
—this, too, had been stripped of everything valuable, and
Peter's eyes swept around, making sure there was nothing
left to steal.

Then he said: "Where did Lara get it? Mother's chain?"

Angel was relieved, if that was all he had found. "I gave
it to her." She even somewhat took the offensive: "I
thought it was mine to give to whoever I want."

"Mother often wore that chain. I think it was her
mother's, or was it her grandmother's? Anyway, it was from
that side of the family."

"So it's all right if it goes to *my* side of the family,"
Angel tried to make a joke of it. "And Lara loves it so
much, she never takes it off—"

"She was asleep," Peter interrupted.

Angel tried to sound casual: "Did she wake up?"

"No." He frowned. "I tried to wake her, but it was—
she was—does she take anything? Any pills or anything?"

Angel understood his deep unease, for she herself had
on occasion tried to rouse Lara from a deep, drugged sleep.
It was eerie the way it was impossible to get through to her:
she was not like Lara at all, but heavy, inert, inhuman, like a
cloth doll with dangling limbs.

"She wasn't wearing any clothes," Peter said. "She
wasn't wearing anything except Mother's chain. . . .
What if someone else had come in?"

"Who?" Angel laughed it off. "No one else has the key
—only you and I."

"What if something happened?"

"Like what? What could happen?"

"If she took too many pills by mistake."

"But who says she takes anything? Except yes, a sleep-ing pill now and again because she gets restless at night and keeps me awake."

Peter walked up and down a bit, frowning to himself, checked his mother's closets, then came back to Angel and stood in front of her: "What about you?" he said. She gazed at him in polite inquiry. "Don't you think you're spending too much time looking after other people? First your mother, then your cousin." Angel continued to look up at him, her eyes unblinking and owllike behind her glasses. Perhaps to evade this look, he moved away from her again. He said very calmly: "I know it was I who asked you to go and live with her, but now I see it wasn't the best solution for anyone. I feel rather guilty about it," he said, still very calm and conveying no sense of guilt.

"Oh," said Angel, also calm, "I did it for myself, not for you."

He began to open and shut the drawers of his mother's dresser, checking up on the contents. Then he said, "What's the matter with her anyway? Why is she so—"

"Nervous? Well—I guess she's going through a kind of phase—we all do, don't we—she'll be all right once she starts working again. At her dancing," she said. "She really misses it."

"Of course the apartment is yours, you know that," Peter said. "I bought it in your name. . . . That's what I keep telling Lilian: surely I can go visit my own daughter in her own apartment? But Lilian can be very unreasonable— once she gets an idea in her head, there's nothing I can do to talk her out of it." He shut the last drawer, satisfied that the dresser contained nothing more valuable than his mother's underclothes. "Well, at any rate, she's done a good job of clearing out the apartment," he said in commendation of his wife. "I only wish she could have gotten here before the watch and bracelet disappeared—"

"What about Rose?"

"We'll find her. Or, rather, the police will." At the expression on her face, he continued, "Unlike you, Angel, I don't intend to sit still and let people take whatever they like from me."

They were interrupted by the door opening—"We have to use the little girl's room." It was the nurse leading Grandmother Koenig—very slowly, so as to share in whatever conversation might be going on. When Peter and Angel were silent, she herself began to talk to Grandmother Koenig, commenting on the family photographs displayed around the bedroom. These were a recent addition—Peter at his prep school, Grandfather Koenig vacationing in the South of France, Lilian and the boys—piously put up by Lilian in place of the paintings and other valuables now in storage. The nurse clucked and admired, but her patient remained impassive, refusing to recognize anyone except a Siamese cat called China.

Peter waited for them to disappear into the bathroom before commenting about the nurse: "Lilian got her from a good agency, but of course you can't trust them further than you can see them. . . . Still, it's the best solution under the circumstances. Mother is comfortable and at the same time the apartment is being kept clean and looked after—we all know what happens to places when they're left empty with only a cleaning woman or someone like what's-her-name—"

"Rose. She probably thought it was just costume jewelry. Anyway, I don't believe she took it at all."

But Peter was not inclined to discuss Rose. Instead, he said, "There wouldn't be the same problem with your place. There's nothing in it worth a dime, so you could just lock it up and walk away if you wanted to. You have to be careful about renting to a tenant, though; best is simply to leave it to appreciate till you're ready to put it on the market. *If* you ever want to sell, Angel. It's entirely up to you, as I say."

ROLAND, LOOKING GRIM, was with Lara, who was laughing at him. But when Angel came in, she said quickly, "Don't tell her." And at once that fear gripped Angel again, of unknown cause.

"I have to tell her."

"Why? It was a joke. . . . And you can take it back if you want, it's just junk, though I paid for it."

"Did you?" Roland said gravely.

From the back of her closet where she had hidden it, she took out a shopping bag and, one by one, began to toss out the contents. It *was* junk, really nothing anyone would need—but pretty, like everything that Lara had: a silk sash, a velvet pouch, a painted picture frame, small desirable useless things from the gift department. With each one she threw out, she said, "I paid."

Roland said to Angel, "I don't know what would have

happened if my friend hadn't been working in the store. He knew her. They all know her in that store from when she lived in the hotel and was in and out of there every day, buying things and taking them back. I promised someone'd come pay for the stuff, so it's okay—but what if it happens somewhere else?"

Lara flung herself on her futon, on her stomach and her face buried in her arms.

"You'd be in a lot of trouble," Roland told her. "With the police and the court and lawyers and all of that."

"Rub my back," said Lara in a plaintive, muffled voice.

"And the psychiatrists and the hospitals. You wouldn't like it." He got down to massage her spine, at the same time looking up at Angel, both of them helpless and responsible.

Angel said, "Who should I pay?"

"I paid—I paid," said Lara, not raising her head but kicking out with one leg for emphasis.

"My friend took it on his account and you can write a check to him."

"I'll do it now." Angel went into the other bedroom to get her checkbook. She half hoped that if she paid off at once, with no delay, it might all go away and be as though it had not happened. But before she could return to ask the friend's name and the amount to be filled in, she heard their raised voices—Lara's in fury and Roland defending himself. She was tempted not to go back in but to let Roland deal with her on his own—just this once, for someone else to do so instead of herself. But next moment she had overcome this temptation and was in the room with them.

Lara was sitting up on her futon, supported on one

hand; her dress had slipped off one shoulder and her hair was tumbled about her face. Roland had distanced himself from her and stood pressed against the opposite wall, staring at her. She was shouting with her mouth wide open, revealing the gap where a tooth had gone in her lower jaw. Never for one moment, she said, had she held it against him that he was only a waiter in the hotel where she had lived as a guest—that was a matter of complete indifference to her as long as she believed him to be what he had pretended: a good guy and a friend. But she should have let herself be warned by her own instincts which had always been repelled by him—for instance, by his smell and cheap nasty little underpants he wore. She noticed at once that these physical details upset him more than anything, so she continued in that strain. He got away from her as far as he could, backed right against the wall, while she said how she felt like throwing up every time he came near her let alone got into bed with her. Always pale-complexioned, his face was now stark white and at the same time he attempted to smile to show that he was not taking her seriously but pitied her. Yet it was he who looked pitiful. Angel wanted to help him, only she knew that any interference would drive Lara further and perhaps make her turn against Angel too. So Angel said nothing, intending in some way to make it up to Roland at some future time.

However, the moment he had gone, Angel saw that she was still holding the check she had to give him. She went after him immediately, but when she got down, he had already left the building. She followed him into the street, and on a guess she turned right and began to run and call;

she must have looked odd, but no one took any notice. He was standing waiting to cross by the intersection, and just as she reached him the lights changed, so she caught his sleeve to hold him back. "Don't touch me," he threatened her, but when she showed him the check, he told her how to fill it in. She did so there and then on the sidewalk, and when she gave it to him, she said, "I'm sorry." He laughed in a shrill, simulated way: "I don't believe it: she's sorry." Only his laughter was simulated—when he thrust his face down into hers, it was charged with true emotion: *"I'm* sorry," he said fiercely. "For you: I feel sorry for you." Then he left her and crossed the street, though the red sign had begun to flash. Watching him walk away, very stiff and proud but with his thin shoulder blades twitching, Angel knew that he would not look back and that they would not see him again.

Many years later Roland said, "I did feel sorry for her, and I even thought I'd turn back, to warn her or something. Afterward I wish I had, but at the time I was thankful to get out myself and be free of that situation. Anyhow, you can't help other people, I learned that long ago. They have to do what they think they have to do."

THE NEXT TIME Lara was caught shoplifting, she was again reprieved—this time through Hugo, or, rather, Helgabeth, who happened to be friendly with the design consultant of the store in which the incident occurred. Helgabeth went rushing around there and diplomatically settled matters (a donation to charity was involved). Afterward she said to Hugo and Angel: "It's completely ridiculous to let her run around the city as though she were a healthy person."

"I can understand that you won't treat her yourself," she told Hugo, "but good heavens, we're living in the twentieth century, people are no longer locked up at home in the care of their relatives. If you had heard the scene I had in the store this afternoon—very well, luckily she was my friend, but it was not easy, I can tell you, they have too many of these cases and have to protect themselves. And no one is speaking of prison or anything like that but of treatment, doctors, and hospitals, what's wrong with that when it is necessary—necessary—necessary."

She paused to collect herself. Then she came up behind Hugo and laid her hand on his shoulder: "And what about this great man?" she said in her deep, rich, strangely accented voice that made everything she said portentous. "We can't have him distracted from his work but all must pull together to relieve him of common worries. All right, my darling, I won't say any more, but you and Angel must talk together and make a decision—no, don't thank me: it's not only as your friend that I have helped, but for the sake of your precious work." She kissed the top of his head and tactfully left them alone together.

Hugo said, "What do you want to do?"

"What we have been doing," said Angel, making herself sound cheerful and stouthearted.

"Yes, but should I allow you to? . . . You heard what Helena said—accused me of—and rightly: in all this, we haven't thought about *you*."

"Well, please don't." Angel smiled deprecatingly.

"Mother has this obsession about some great work that I'm neglecting. I don't like to disillusion her, but believe me, there is no such thing."

"How could there be in the life you've been having with Lara?" But when he continued, it was about himself: "I used to get these phone calls, and it might be from anywhere in the world. From Lara's boarding school to say she'd been expelled and where should we send her; or she'd be visiting Alice in her commune or clinic or wherever she'd checked herself in and they'd have one of their ghastly fights and Alice would go off and commit suicide, or try to."

After the briefest pause Angel said, "Those pills you prescribed? They're making her sleep too much."

"How long do you think you can carry on with pills?"

Angel had gotten up and stood planted sturdily in front of him, with her halo of curly hair. Her posture and her silence made it clear that there was no argument, or that she was beyond it. Hugo took out his prescription pad and, after some questions, wrote out what she wanted. Angel put it away carefully and said, to comfort him: "She'll get better."

Hugo walked with her to the door. He wanted to say something more—probably on a personal level, but when he spoke, it was about his work. Angel was grateful to him for letting them be and also for the prescription, so she listened with a show of interest while he told her about human perfectibility and the standards he was trying to set up: to show that this is what people are, but this is what they could be.

4

THINKING ABOUT ROSE, Angel wondered where she had gone and if she could find her anywhere. She telephoned the agency who had originally sent her, but she had not reported back to them after leaving Grandmother Koenig's. Angel hoped that this meant Rose was not in urgent need of earning money. Perhaps she even had enough to rent a room in some hotel that was not too dangerous or dirty. Rose had told her that some of these places were so bad that it was better to be out in the street, at least when the weather was warm. This, too, she had done, packing her belongings in a little cart and sheltering in the doorway of the kitchen and back entrance of a Chinese restaurant. They hadn't liked her being there, but they had given her leftover food for a while. Then the health department had come and closed down the Chinese kitchen and moved Rose to a shelter for women, where she had stayed till she could afford another hotel room. She had a brother living with his girlfriend in Brooklyn, but the atmosphere in their house was very bad for her, with a lot of drinking and other dangerous influences she was trying to get away from. Before going to Grandmother Koenig, she had been in a hostel run for and by ex-alcoholics— Angel found the telephone number, but they, too, knew nothing of her. Perhaps Grandmother Koenig's bracelet and watch were helping to support her, though for how long would depend on how much she could get for them: it was unlikely that Rose knew, or that anyone would give her, anywhere near the right price.

Angel's vision of the city, formed from within her grandparents' house, had always been beatific. Perched in her attic room, she had looked down into the little paved garden with the stone nymph, or up toward the brilliant new towers rising above and around her. And in the streets, too, she had tended to look upward to where artificial and heavenly light together formed a fabulously shifting panorama, and the only reason to look down was to see its reflection shimmering in the depths of the river, dirty but, in the dark, romantic. Lately she had begun to have a different vision of her city: of Rose adrift in the streets, dragging her belongings behind her on her little cart; or in some pawnshop being cheated of the jewelry she had stolen. And, equally adrift, Lara picking up strangers in the middle of Broadway, or stalking in a department store between glass counters full of baubles shining at her like real gold. And let alone the public places, the lobby of their building was as open as the streets, and in spite of the high-tech security system, access to their apartment seemed to involve no more than pushing a button in an elevator: anyone could do that and go up and open the door where Lara was and find her naked, or asleep, or God knew in what mood or mind.

Helena remembered the day Angel told her that she wanted to move Lara into the house. She remembered in detail everything that happened during those days, having spent the rest of her life repeating it in her mind. She said how surprised she was when she came home in the evening to find Angel still in the office—nowadays she always left early, in fact, earlier and earlier every day. Helena had gone down and Angel said, with no preliminaries: "You know what we talked about the other day? About Lara and me moving into the house?"

To gain time, Helena had slowly removed her hat and coat and put them down on a chair and drawn up another chair for herself. She answered: "That's not what we talked about." She reminded her: "We talked about the Aroras moving in. You said you'd think about it."

"I know that—but we also—"

"No, we did not, darling."

Angel looked at her watch, making it clear that she had no time to argue. Instead, she became angry with her mother: "You'd rather have those people here than Lara and me." When Helen could only shake her head in denial, she raised her voice: "They have absolutely no right to be here, and you have no right to bring them here. Because it's not only your house, it's ours too, Lara's and mine."

Anger was not anything innate in Angel, it was more like a blight on her true nature, obscuring it like algae or some other fungus on clear water. Her face at that moment was also marred, it was flushed, damp, and ugly, so that Helena had to avert her eyes from her. Taking her mother's silence for resistance, Angel told her: "There's no point in talking anymore—if we want to move in, you can't stop us."

Her eyes still lowered away from Angel, Helena began, "I don't want to—" meaning "I don't want to stop you," but Angel interpreted it as "I don't want you here" and said grimly, "We'll see about that," and made to leave. Helena jumped up and tried to explain, but Angel had no time to listen. Helena became desperate, she thought if they could only talk the way they used to, they would regain some of their understanding; but Angel would not be delayed another minute, and she said, "Can't you see—I have to get *home,* why are you in my way?" She pushed her mother aside and ran out. Left alone, Helena sank down on an office chair and covered her face with her hands. She didn't know what had happened, why everything had changed, why they lived in darkness.

Afterward Helena tried to explain it like this: "She had so utterly given herself over to one person that everything else, the whole world, all of us—her own self—everything was dead for her." She stared into space with her own dead eyes—this was in one of those dark, unaired apartments she inhabited after she sold the house.

WHEN ANGEL RAN from the house, it was with feelings of anger for what lay behind her and of anxiety for what lay before her. Helena had delayed her too long! A

bus drew up near her and she jumped on, but it was stuck
in traffic so she got off again and continued half running,
half walking, pushing through the crowd. In a narrow cleft
between the clifflike buildings, the sun was extinguishing
itself in its own lake of fire; an almost full moon had been
prematurely switched on along with the commercial signs.
Angel saw nothing—she kept looking at her watch, kept
muttering to herself as in prayer: "Let her be home."

But when she got there, it was as she had feared, and
the apartment was empty. In Lara's room her futon was left
open and covered with various outfits that Lara had tried
on and discarded. Several pairs of shoes were scattered
about, and jars and bottles were left unstoppered, releasing
their perfumes. Lara must have planned to go on some very
special expedition to be so eager to dress up for it; only
where could that be, Angel thought, folding and replacing
the clothes flung about, and with whom? They knew so
few people; in all this big city, besides a few casual acquaintances, Lara had only Angel herself, and Hugo, and Helena,
who disliked her. Again Angel's anger rose against her
mother, on several counts now, but she suppressed it to
concentrate on the more important thought of where to
find Lara. She considered calling Hugo but decided against
it at once: Lara would not have dressed up only to go and
see her father. Angel blamed herself—it was Helena's fault,
but she should not have allowed herself to be delayed, no,
not even by, what was it? Fifteen minutes? Twenty? Certainly less than half an hour. It seemed a short time, but
perhaps not short at all to someone alone at home and
waiting; and how sweet it was, Angel thought, to be waited
for like that, the way Lara did for her. And then to have

failed her—Angel's heart was torn and she buried her face in the garment she was folding to tidy away.

She went out to look for her. First, with an overbright smile, she asked the receptionists and doormen if they had happened to see her leave, but no one had, most of them having only just come on duty. She left the building to walk down the street and into the main avenue. By now the crowds were not office workers on their way home but people eager for their evening's entertainment. The restaurants at the four corners of the intersecting streets were all full, their glass walls giving a view deep into their interiors, where mirrors redoubled the buffet sideboards and waiters jostling each other with their shoulder-borne trays. One of the restaurants spilled onto the sidewalk with more tables railed off by banks of flowers, and although it was not very warm outside, these, too, were full and everyone in a hurry to eat, for the shows and concerts were about to start. Already lines had formed outside the cinemas, music lovers were waiting for each other on the steps of the concert halls, and the doors of the opera house stood open to the Chagall mural and the red plush stairs inside. Angel passed a tall, handsome girl, not unlike Lara but surrounded by friends—perhaps it was her birthday, for she was holding flowers wrapped in cellophane with multicolored ribbons. When Angel came to a flower shop, she went in and bought not one but two bouquets, and then she stood in line in their favorite delicatessen and bought all the things Lara liked best. By the time she came out, it was quite late and no doubt Lara was home and wondering and worrying what had happened to her. Angel began to hurry but was stopped at a corner by a man needing the price of a cup of coffee, and it took Angel some time to get at her change because of the flowers and containers she was holding. Only a few yards farther on, sheltering in the doorway of a bakery, now dark and shut until early morning, she saw a thin youngish woman with two paper sacks packed neatly right to the top; she didn't ask for anything but sat staring in front of her, cocooned in silence.

Arriving in the brightly lit lobby of her building, she resisted the temptation to ask the receptionist if he had seen Lara come home. Even if he said no, it wouldn't mean anything, because he might very well have missed her with all the people emerging from the elevators, dressed up for their evening dates, and others, equally fresh and eager, surging in to join some party upstairs. There were several partygoers in the elevator with Angel, carrying bottles of wine, and because she, too, was festively laden, they expected her to get off on the same floor; but she went farther up, alone now, telling herself she's sure to be home. When she got off and turned down the corridor, she heard a phone ring—it rang and no one picked it up, and when she reached the door, it was still ringing and it was her phone. She dropped her packets and flowers to get at her key, and in her nervousness fumbled around the lock, thinking how the phone ringing didn't mean there was no one to answer it because often Lara didn't bother. Getting the door open at last, Angel called "Lara!" quite expecting her to be there, and at the same time ran to the phone.

It was Lilian, and Angel surmised at once that something had happened to Grandmother Koenig. Now her mind was divided in anxiety over her grandmother and over Lara, who was surely in the bedroom (she put her hand over the mouthpiece and called again "Lara!"). Lilian was saying, "She's here," and Angel said "Where?" thinking how could Grandmother Koenig escape from her nurse and get on the train to Peter's house. "Here—here—here," Lilian said, desperation mixed with rage. "She says she wants to see Peter. You'd better come and get her." "Of course I will," Angel said, "but couldn't she stay the night with you?" "Stay the night! Are you as insane as your cousin?" So it was not Grandmother Koenig who had gotten on the train to go and see Peter.

WHEN ANGEL GOT off at the station, the local cab driver she hired was no longer the one they had met before. This one seemed hardly old enough to have qualified for a license: he had no answer to Angel's questions about the other driver, in fact was totally disinclined to conversation, drowning it out with loud music as he drove wildly around the bends of the country roads. Lilian was waiting on her porch: she wore a short velvet evening dress with a bouffant skirt and was very, very agitated. So was Angel, who asked at once, "Where is she?" "She's asleep," said Lilian in disgust. After the last few hours this was an anticlimax, and Angel laughed, so Lilian became more furious: "You'd better get her out of here fast, because I'm expecting guests."

Lara's sleep didn't appear drug induced but as though she had just dropped off after an exhausting day. She was sitting upright on a sofa with one hand laid in her lap, and Angel, carefully sitting down next to her, laid her own on top of it. She was so glad to have found her, she forgot everything—including where they were, in Lilian's best room. This was done up in a domino theme of black and white cubes and had been featured in magazines. The house was very modern and quite different from Grandmother Koenig's baroque residence; and yet there was something that instantly recalled that establishment—a sense that things came first and were there to be cherished and served by the people who had the good fortune to live among them.

Lilian, teetering on the too-high heels she wore to make herself a bit taller, stood in front of the two girls and said they must leave now, quickly; and when Angel put her finger on her lips, Lilian repeated *"Now,"* in a whisper. She was distracted by her maid entering with a cart of canapés, which she wheeled in the wrong place. This maid was Hispanic and young, but Lilian's tone with her was the same as Grandmother Koenig's had been with her old Teutonic maid, assuming that unless watched by an expert eye, she would commit every error in the book, and very likely on purpose.

There was the sound of a car outside—Lilian warned, "It's Peter," and hurried out to meet him. Angel continued to sit peacefully beside Lara. She exchanged smiles with the maid, who offered her some canapés, and Angel accepted, for she hadn't eaten and was hungry. Probably Lara was too —Angel whispered in her ear to wake her and, moaning a bit to be disturbed, Lara opened her eyes: "Why are you here?" she said to Angel, but at the sight of the canapés said at once she was starving. The maid filled a whole plate of them and giggled to see them eat so hungrily. Outside, arguing voices could be heard, principally Lilian's, till at last

Peter said, "But where are they?" His firm footsteps approached the room and next moment he was in it. Lilian came up behind him and gasped to see the two of them eating up her party food. The maid went away, while the two girls lowered their heads and continued eating, not knowing what else to do.

Peter said at once, "I'll drive you to the station."

Lara looked up at him, made her eyes swim: "Why can't we stay for your party?"

Angel said, "I'm not really dressed for a dinner party."

"When are you ever?" joked Peter, grateful for her help. Then he appealed to her: "Let me take you."

Angel got up, but Lara continued to sit there, hopefully looking up at the three of them to be allowed to stay. No one could say she wasn't dressed for a party. She shone splendidly in a rose-colored, tight-fitting, low-cut dress, with bracelets on her arms, long earrings, and several chains around her neck, including Grandmother Koenig's. Peter couldn't help himself from visibly admiring her; his face wore the wistful, flushed, boyish look it had when he desired something very much. She smiled at him: "I want to stay."

Peter might have been tempted to smile back at her, to say "Stay, if you want." But there was Lilian, and she, too, had flushed, and she said to Peter in a voice as tense and tight as her face: "If you're going to the station, you'd better do it, don't you think." Peter stopped gazing at Lara and said he would. But still Lara didn't move; she was still smiling, and only Angel noticed that her face was slightly askew.

Peter appealed to Angel: "I've got the car outside."

Lilian said, "There's a train in twenty minutes, you'll just make it."

Angel looked at the two of them standing side by side: Lilian, small and steely, was determined to clear out her house for her dinner guests, while Peter, even if he had other desires, was there to give her his sturdy support to preserve the sanctity of their social life. Together, they were absolutely capable of dealing with the situation. It wasn't even all that new to them—they had seen people "flip out" before, as they called it, including one or two from their own circle who had suddenly swallowed sleeping pills or shouted obscenities on the golf course. When that happened, it was someone's responsibility to take them away somewhere to receive proper treatment.

Conscious of the charge of power in these two, Angel was equally conscious of Lara's, and more afraid of it. She knew how unpredictable was her next mood, the next beat of her blood. It wasn't only the danger from outside—that someone might say or do something to disturb her—but the malfunction within her that could suddenly throw her out of gear.

Peter said to Angel, "Come on, I'll take you," no longer in appeal.

Angel sat down next to Lara again. She began to stroke her sleeve—through the silk Lara's arm felt full and firm and warm—trying to communicate to her that whatever happened she, Angel, was there with her and for her.

Now Peter stood in front of Lara and held out his hand to her with fingers playfully beckoning, as to a child. It may have been his kindliness, or it may have been Angel's, that

made Lara docilely take his hand to help her up. They all
went out to Peter's car still parked by the porch, and while
he settled the two girls in the backseat, Lilian warned him
to drive straight home again to shower and change. Before
they drove off, she just had time to thrust her head through
the window: "Where did she get that?" she asked Angel,
but Lara at once put her hand over Grandmother Koenig's
chain and kept it there till they were out of sight.

Although he had been very calm, even a little paternal,
up till then, as soon as he was behind the wheel Peter drove
as wildly as the teenage cab driver. Angel stretched out her
hand to prevent Lara from being thrown forward—but suddenly, thrusting that protective hand away, Lara lunged forward to clasp her arms around Peter's neck. The car skidded
and, with a driver less in control, might have done worse;
Peter gripped the wheel and his voice shook only a little as
he said, "Whoa, Lara, you nearly had us in the ditch there."

Lara cried into his ear, "Come with us!"

"I'll come tomorrow," said Peter with remarkable
composure. "I'll see you in town." When she tightened her
grip on him, he slowed down, ready and alert at any second
to slam on the brake. His voice continued absolutely calm
and reasonable: "If you don't let go, Lara, I can't drive."

She began to shower him with kisses. His whole head
was in a deep flush—probably he had high blood pressure,
and no wonder with those rich meals he had eaten all his
life long—but he continued driving steadily, determined to
get them to the station, out of his car and on to the train.

Angel also saw that this was the only solution and tried
to help him. To draw her off, she put her arms around
Lara's waist. Lara ignored her, intent only on Peter, whis-

pering into his ear. Angel laid her head tenderly on Lara's back, her arms still holding on to her unyielding waist.

Suddenly she felt herself flung against the backseat. She had succeeded in diverting Lara from Peter, only to draw her force on to herself. Lara put one hand on Angel's throat and pressed it without a word, and without a word or sound Angel struggled to get free. This went on for some time, Lara intent on hurting Angel and Angel on defending herself, and both of them in utter silence, as though wanting to keep what they were doing from Peter. They were helped by Peter himself, who went on driving; if he knew anything of the silent struggle going on behind him, he kept his manly back turned on it.

It was an unequal struggle, since Lara, who was stronger anyway, was now fueled by a more powerful emotion than Angel, who wanted only to save herself. But it was Peter who saved her: swinging into the station yard, he jumped out without turning off the engine and, opening the back door for them—"Quick!" he cried. "You'll just make it." He didn't look at either of them but strained into the distance, in the direction from which the train was due. "Have you got the money for the tickets? You're all right, then." He got back in the driver's seat, idling the engine for a moment. "It'll be here any minute," he promised. "You won't have to wait. Anyhow, I'll see you both tomorrow." He took his foot off the clutch, releasing the engine and himself.

Lara and Angel walked quietly and side by side into the station waiting room. Angel could not speak, she felt there was a wound inside her throat. She tried to relieve it by clearing it, but the pain increased; fearing a visible bruise, she put up her hand to hold it against her neck. Lara was completely subdued; she willingly sat on the bench Angel indicated and folded her hands in her lap. Angel went into the ladies' room; it was empty, but she could see a pair of feet under the stall, so she was as quiet as possible as she regurgitated over the washbasin. When she heard the flush, she straightened up and saw herself in the mirror, where she looked quite normal except for a reddened mark on her neck. A woman came out of the stall and washed in the basin next to Angel; she commented on the train being late again and how someone ought to do something. Angel smiled assent and went into the stall; she tried to lock it, but the catch was gone. When she heard the woman leave, she sank to the ground and retched into the toilet bowl and then remained kneeling there with her head over it. Although the rest-room fittings were old and old-fashioned, the little gray and black tiles were scrupulously scrubbed and everything was saturated in disinfectant. Now Angel was sobbing more than retching, and with her tears flowing into the bowl, she despaired of what to do and how to carry on by herself; she felt she could not—not even as much as getting Lara back to town. But when she heard someone enter, she got up off the floor and went out. She kept her head averted, waiting for the woman to enter the stall, then turned on the tap and thoroughly washed her face and dried it on a paper towel. The pain in her throat was subsiding; it was bearable.

When she came out of the rest room, she looked toward the place where she had left Lara. It was empty. Angel panicked, and again the idea that she could not go on, carry on by herself, took possession of her. She glanced around the waiting room—and saw Lara sitting in another place, with a magazine and a packet of chocolate-covered raisins she had bought from the little newsstand. Reading and eating, she appeared contented. The few other waiting passengers—the woman who had been in the rest room, a man with a crutch, an exhausted girl with a baby in a knitted cap —threw curious glances at her, brilliant in her shining pink dress and jewelry. Angel turned away; she knew she would have to join her but felt reluctant and was glad that there was the business of buying their tickets. When that was finished, she walked slowly toward Lara and with each step she thought, I can't. But Lara made an inviting gesture of moving over, though there was plenty of room on the bench, and when Angel had sat down next to her, she offered her the chocolate-covered raisins, solicitously tilting the package to let them slide out.

PETER DID NOT keep his promise of visiting them the next day, but he telephoned Angel in the office: "We tracked down that woman, what's her name, the one who walked off with Mother's jewelry."

"Rose? . . . You don't know that she walked off with anything."

In no mood to argue, he changed the subject: "Lilian says if you want help with moving, she'll be glad to give you a hand."

"Oh," said Angel, "you know how we really don't have that much stuff."

"Well, if you want her, she's there. Wouldn't take her a

minute—you've seen how good she is at clearing out places."

When Angel arrived at Helena's house, her mother was out and she found only Rohit there. He had brought a little dish from his mother and invited Angel to taste—"It's not very hot," he promised, and then they both smiled, remembering their first meeting when she had burned her palate on his lamb curry. Now Angel blamed herself not even to have noticed how long it was since they had met. But Rohit blamed himself: he said how much he had missed her, but nowadays, as soon as he was off duty, he had to go apartment-hunting. Yes, perhaps Angel hadn't heard, he and his mother had to move, their lease was expiring and the landlord was putting up the rent exorbitantly. They would have liked to find something in this neighborhood, but prices were too high, so they would have to accept the offer of some Indian friends of an upstairs flat in their house in Queens. He said how sorry they were that they could not remain nearer to Helena, and Angel agreed it was a pity; she added, "So it's just as well I'm moving back in here."

Rohit's eyes lit up, he exclaimed, "Oh, but how wonderful!"

"Yes, Lara and I both," said Angel. "I thought you were going to let me taste that curry."

He ladled some out for her and she ate and praised it. He thanked her without looking at her, his eyes downcast. He was in his airlines uniform, and it made him look even more boyish, as though dressed for school. To Angel it seemed that they had spent their carefree youth together.

But she had no time or taste for nostalgia, and deciding she could not wait for Helena, she said good-bye to Rohit. He said he would go with her. She didn't want his company, but he doggedly followed her, and waited for the crosstown bus with her. When it came, he asked her for a token and she paid it for him and they stood wedged side by side hanging on to straps. They were lucky, two people got off just where they were standing, Angel sat down and Rohit with her. Quite against his usual custom, he pretended not to see the elderly woman who had been hoping for the seat and now stood swaying above him. But he felt guilty, and it was now necessary for him to be engrossed in conversation with Angel. He spoke in a low voice, but she could hear clearly, for it was right into her ear; she had her head turned away and looked out the window as they went through the park, where the leaves looked metallic with the streetlights shining up into them.

Rohit told her how as a little boy he would sit for hours in his mother's lap while she stroked his hair and wound it around her fingers: till suddenly she grew tense, and then Rohit would climb out of her lap so that she could go and see what Vikram was doing. She was always uncertain about this elder son, and Rohit, too, did not know what to expect of him. Often his brother was kind and bought him ice lollies on sticks, and plastic toys. But sometimes he was bored and in need of amusement: there was the time when he gave Rohit a pair of scissors to stick into an electric outlet. Rohit said that the shock that had at that moment passed through him had never gone away—yes, even now, he said, right into Angel's ear as though wishing to penetrate her with the same current of fear, many years after his brother's death he could still feel it.

The bus had wound its way through the park and come out the other end, and although she still had one stop to go, Angel said she wanted to get off. He went with her, but when they were in the street, she asked him not to come any farther. But he did so all the same, still talking about his brother. If he had done this to relieve his own feelings, she would have been willing to listen, but he was doing it to influence hers. He said his brother and a group of friends had stolen cars, stolen money from guests and servants and elderly relatives, had poisoned dogs for barking at them. All these were considered adolescent exploits, and it was true that most of the friends had grown out of them and had gone on to college and good careers. Vikram had found other friends, strange characters not at all like the friends he had gone to school with. Now his activities had brought the police into the house, and several times he was called in for questioning. Each time he swore his innocence, he swore it on his mother's life—his favorite and most irrefutable oath—and she was the first to believe him. Yet the tension Rohit had felt in her at the least stir from his brother had become a permanent part of her and of the whole household. They were always alert—when the telephone rang, or someone knocked on the front door, or at the sound of laughter and good times from Vikram's friends whom he had brought into his room. When Rohit passed that room to get to his own, he did so as silently as possible. Sometimes the door opened and the brother appeared to shout down to the servant for more ice and soda; he looked wild and flushed, and Rohit tried to steal past him. Once his brother saw him and put out his hand and Rohit squeezed himself against the wall—but his brother only wanted to ruffle his hair in a friendly way, saying "Hi, Junior," in the Indo-American accent he had cultivated.

They had reached the corner before Angel's apartment house. Rohit didn't want to go any farther, and they both stood still, looking toward the building, where all the lights were on from the canopy up to the pinnacle that touched the sky. Mixed in with Angel's anxiety to go in and upstairs, there was the opposite desire of turning around and walking away with Rohit. She rested her arms on his shoulders for a moment, in affection or to support herself.

He said, "For years and years Mummy said, 'He'll change, he's only a child, wait till he grows up.' But it got worse; worse and worse," he whispered. But she took her arms off his shoulders, her moment of friendship was over, she said good-bye and set off for her building.

LARA MAY HAVE been lurking inside their door, for as soon as Angel entered she came flying out at her— "Where have you been? Why have you left me alone so long?" Instinctively, Angel put up her arm to guard her head. Lara laughed and drew back: "Did you think I was going to hit you?"

Angel took off her coat and hung it up. She affected calm; inwardly she exhorted herself, let me do this right. If she did, everything would be fine—and Lara would be gentle and good company for the rest of the evening.

She stepped up close again—this time Angel willed herself not to flinch, although again she did not know what Lara intended. Probably Lara didn't know either; her lip trembled, she appeared to be asking for help. She said, "I called Peter today—what could I do! He hasn't been to see me and you weren't home—"

"I was in the office, you could have called me."

She shrugged. "Anyway, he wasn't home. *She* was."

"Lilian? . . . What did she say?"

"She said, 'You're sick, you should check yourself into the hospital and have treatment.' "

Angel said, quite slowly and sensibly, "I think it's better if you don't call their house again or go there or anything. Lilian is different from us. I'm not saying she's better or worse or whatever, but she doesn't understand us, that's all."

"You and she are the same. You also think I'm crazy and want to put me in the hospital."

Angel clasped Lara's wrist—it was a protective gesture, but Lara made out that it was a restraining one and broke free. She ran into the bathroom and locked the door. Angel could hear her rummaging inside the bathroom cabinet, she was knocking over bottles—"Where do you keep them?" she cried. Bottles crashed to the floor, glass shattered. Angel shouted through the door: "They're not there!"

"Where are they? They're *my* pills."

"I have them. Just come out of there. You know I have them—you gave them to me to keep."

There was a sudden cry from inside. The next moment Lara opened the door and stood there, holding a razor, a gash on her wrist at which she gazed in horror. Angel took the injured wrist. Lara had not gone very deep but probably deeper than she had intended, the razor cutting more sharply than she had expected. She surrendered it at once to Angel, as also her wrist and herself, letting Angel wash the wound and dress it. Angel did all this in the utmost agitation and kept saying why, why, until in the end Lara answered her, "Because I don't want to live anymore."

These hollow words, and the hollow tone in which she spoke them, sank without hindrance to the depth of Angel's soul. The dank sound they made was echoed there. Angel realized that what had once been full was now emptied—the clear running waters of life in which the sky and green leaves and all beautiful things had been mirrored had dried up, leaving only a stagnant puddle that mirrored nothing.

But she said heroically, "I'm never going to leave you alone, ever again. Wherever you are, I'll be with you."

Lara accepted this in silence. She let Angel wash her face, comb her hair, and put her coat on, pulling down the sleeve to hide the bandaged wrist. It was only when they were on their way out that she asked where they were going and seemed to acquiesce when Angel told her they were going to Helena's, to arrange about moving into the house the next day.

TWENTY YEARS LATER, this is how Helena remembered that evening:

"When Angel brought Lara, I at once called Hugo, and we both tried to persuade Lara to go into a hospital. Actually, it wasn't her we were persuading, but Angel, who kept saying, 'It was my fault, my fault.' Hugo warned her that

Lara was going to try this again, but Angel said no, from now on she would take much better care of her, and that she would move her into the house to be with her night and day. Hugo said, 'You may be prepared to take this on, but what about Helena?' Angel promptly replied that yes, she felt guilty about me, and mostly she was moving back so that I wouldn't have to be in the house all alone. (By this time my Angel could lie better than anyone.) Lara took no part in the discussion, she sat huddled on the couch, under my parents' photograph; sometimes she raised her wrist to her mouth and bit irritably at the bandage—like a sick dog, I thought. I felt I couldn't bear to look at her or even to be in the same room with her.

"I went upstairs to get a bedroom ready. It was the same one that Angel and Lara had shared as children. Angel followed me and helped me tuck in the sheets. I said I would get the upstairs room ready for Angel herself, but she said no, she wanted to stay in this one with Lara. She said we could bring in a daybed for her, although as children they had once shared this same bed that we were now making up together. I saw there were tears in her eyes—which was very rare for Angel. I loved her so much, I longed to kiss her sweet face the way I used to. But I could see that she was distracted, her attention all the time on what might be going on in the living room, where Hugo was alone with Lara.

"When we had only half finished the bed, Angel stepped to the window to look down at the stone garden below. I knew what she was thinking and I said it aloud: 'She might try that too,' meaning jump out the window, which Angel understood perfectly though she pretended not to. Then I said, 'Of course I'll do whatever you want, but are you sure we shouldn't do what Hugo says?' She said, 'Wouldn't it be nice if for once you'd do what *I* say,' and she looked at me in that way she now had, as though she hated me. But the next moment she forgot about me, for there were loud cries from the living room and she went rushing down there. Sooner or later I would have to follow her, but I couldn't just yet. I sat on the bed and thought, does she hate me because she thinks I want to have the Aroras here instead of her and Lara? I felt it was all the Aroras' fault, and from that moment I blamed them and began to dislike them for coming between us. I decided at once that I would go down and tell Angel that it was her I wanted here, with her cousin.

"But when I got downstairs, Hugo was standing in the middle of the living room with drops of blood oozing out of a scratch on his cheek. I was shocked, I couldn't speak but only point at his face. He felt it, and then, looking at his fingers, he took out his handkerchief and wiped them off— impatiently, as though it didn't matter very much. By this time Lara was quite calm again and was letting Angel help her wear her coat. Angel said they would be back tomorrow with their things, but before leaving she asked Hugo to write another prescription. He protested that they already had too many pills, but Angel said Lara needed them because he had upset her so badly. Hugo's hand trembled as he wrote; his face was very white, which made the scratch on it stand out. I was so concerned for him that I forgot to tell Angel what I had meant to, about wanting her and Lara here and not the Aroras. By the time I remembered, she had left and without saying good-bye, so that when they didn't return the next day, I blamed myself, to think she felt I didn't want her, and the day after that I decided if they still didn't come I would fetch them myself in the morning, but that was the morning Peter came, bringing the woman with the Polish name who had found them.''

ON THEIR WAY home Angel stopped at a pharmacy to get Hugo's prescription made up, and she hid the new pills in her usual place along with the others. She woke up at night to find Lara rummaging around for them—not at all secretly, but loudly, banging drawers and scrabbling through their contents. When she saw Angel was awake, she demanded, "Where are they?" and "They're mine to take if I need them."

Angel got up and tried to reason with her; but she herself felt that—in face of Lara's stony despair, and her own—her reasons were not good enough. Still she kept on talking, persuading, sometimes both of them sitting on the bed in her room, then in Lara's, finally in the empty dance studio. By then it was about three o'clock in the morning. They felt isolated, sealed off in the apartment, while down below the all-night traffic ebbed and flowed.

Dawn came, and it was a long time since Angel had seen it, for after the restless nights she spent checking up on Lara, she usually slept late. So this first light was all new to her again. By now she had completely run out of arguments—which she didn't believe in the first place—and Lara had kept up her defiance. Angel was exhausted and felt she could do no more. They had reached a dead end.

Then Lara said, "I can do it another way." She began to

push up the lower sash of one of the windows in the studio
—never an easy procedure, and she usually had to call Angel to help her. Today, after some struggle, she managed on
her own, and a current of air, refreshed by dew or a rain
shower somewhere, swept inside the stale room. Lara stood
by the open window, but Angel was not alarmed; she knew
that Lara would have only to glance down into the abyss of
streets below to make her turn away, and this is what happened. But by now Angel knew that Hugo was right and
that she could no longer manage.

Lara changed her approach. She became weak and dependent. She said, "Help me"; she whispered that she was
afraid. She was still determined to do it, saying there was no
other way. Soon Angel would have to call Hugo and ask
him to make the arrangement he had suggested. To prepare
Lara for this departure, she began to pack up their belongings—her own as well, for after giving up Lara, she herself
would move back to Helena's on this same day. Lara followed her around; she was very humble and even helped
fold some of the clothes Angel was packing. But Angel had
to repack them, for Lara had put her own clothes into
Angel's suitcase, not understanding that they would be going to two different places.

By now all the lights had been extinguished in the
buildings as well as the sky; the promise of dawn had not
been fulfilled, and it was a gray, neutral day, neither sun nor
rain. Work in the streets had begun with the pounding of
road drills, and somewhere a burglar alarm or other pierc-
ing sound went off and shrieked ceaselessly. Angel was
ready to shut their two suitcases, when Lara stopped saying,
"Help me." Now she said, "Come with me."

Angel tried to reassure her, she said that although she could not go with her, she would, of course, come to see her often. Lara said, "You'll come to see me?"

"Oh, all the time, every day if they'll let me."

"If who lets you?"

They realized they had been talking at cross-purpose—it was Lara who saw it first, she laughed and said, "No one's going to let you come to see me *there.*" Angel laughed too and blushed for her mistake; but she said, "Don't be silly, Lara."

"It'll be nice to go together," Lara urged. "Anyway, I wouldn't even know which are the right ones or how many to take—I'd do something stupid and just throw up. But you know all those sort of things and you'd do it so well for both of us. . . . Oh, please," she said, and made flirtatious, swimming eyes, the way she did when asking for a favor or a treat.

There was a buzz from downstairs on their intercom. It was nine o'clock in the morning. Lara became deathly pale and said, "Don't answer." But Angel called down to ask who it was. The doorman replied it was a Mrs.—then stopped, made some inquiry, came back: "Mrs. Wisniewski?" sounding dubious both about the name and the person attached to it.

"Hugo has sent them to get me, that's who it is," Lara said. "And you knew about it. You planned it with him."

The doorman buzzed again: "Should I send her up?" Angel called back: "Let me speak to her." Then the visitor came to the intercom and identified herself: it was Rose.

Although Angel convinced Lara that it was not someone sent to take her away, Lara didn't want her to come up.

She said she had to be alone with Angel; no one must come between them.

"I'll see what she wants," Angel pleaded, "and then she'll go and we can be alone together and talk."

"About that?" Lara asked.

After a moment Angel said, "Yes, about that."

"As soon as she's gone?" When Angel felt compelled to agree, Lara said, "All right, remember: you promised." She came up close to her; she kissed her, fastening her mouth on Angel's the way she had done only twice before. This third time Angel felt nothing except the desolation seeping up from the dank, blind place within herself. Lara went into her bedroom and shut the door.

Rose came up, and to apologize for keeping her waiting, Angel said, "I didn't know you were called Mrs. Wisniewski."

"It was that Polish sadist I was married to," Rose explained laconically. Besides her name, she herself was hard to recognize. She was in what must have been quite a fashionable suit before being bought and sold through thrift shops; she wore a muffler and at least two sweaters, though the weather was not yet very cold. She had a little shopping cart packed high with clothes, shoes, and newspapers. Her formerly pasty face had the healthy, weathered color of someone who spends a great deal of time outdoors.

She told Angel that she had been alloted a room in a welfare hotel but had given it up when her brother warned her that the police had come to his place to inquire about her. It was then that she had resumed her married name; and also, not daring to be registered under any address, she had moved partly into the streets, and partly into Grand

Central Station, where she used the washroom and also knew a few people from earlier times she had spent there. But now, after being so happy with Grandmother Koenig, she couldn't take that way of life anymore; and while it was true that through no fault of her own she had been in police trouble before, it was unbearable for her to be a wanted person again—and moreover for something that was not a criminal act on her part but one of friendship and love. She wore a pouch slung around herself out of which she took a plastic bag containing Grandmother Koenig's diamond bracelet and fob-watch. She asked Angel to give them back to Peter so that he could withdraw the police report he had so unfairly made against her.

"She gave them to me," Rose declared, looking straight at Angel to show she wasn't lying. "I said, 'Mrs. Koenig, are you sure?' and she said, 'Yes, Rose, my dear, I'm sure.' " She surrendered the plastic bag to Angel: "I've been carrying them around with me and it never crossed my mind to sell them, except if there was an emergency and I got very sick or something."

All this time there had been no sound from Lara's bedroom. Angel told Rose that she wanted to put the jewelry away for Peter, so she took it into the bedroom and shut the door. She was amazed to find Lara fast asleep. She was lying on her back on her futon, where she had dropped in fatigue. Her breasts, with Grandmother Koenig's chain nestling between them, were breathing gently up and down. Angel was irritated by Lara's ability to go off to sleep so peacefully; but at the same time she realized it was due to the complete trust she had in Angel to take care of everything for both of them. Angel knelt down to undo the clasp of the chain. Then she remembered something else; and rummaging for it in a drawer, she found the pearl brooch she had once given Lara. Helena had been so angry, but in fact Lara had never liked it much and had hardly ever worn it.

Angel insisted that Rose take both the brooch and the chain in exchange for the jewelry she had returned. She placed them in Rose's palm and closed her fingers over them; she offered to give her a note to say that these were a gift so that Rose should feel secure in their possession. At last Rose agreed to take them—because Angel really wanted her to have them, and to please her. It was how she had accepted Grandmother Koenig's jewelry: because it was in the same spirit as Angel's that it had been given, or would have been if Grandmother Koenig had still been her old self. "She'd have said it herself," Rose said. " 'Take them, Rose, because of all you've done for me.' That was the sort of person she was in her heart." She went on to tell some anecdote to illustrate Grandmother Koenig's kindness —in which Angel did not recognize her grandmother's character but was glad to hear her spoken of with such affection.

Angel asked Rose to do her a favor: to come to the apartment and look around to make sure that everything was all right after she and Lara had moved out. "This place isn't right for us," she said, "so we're leaving."

Rose, gazing about the room, said it could be nice with some furniture and rugs on the floor. Angel explained that they had wanted to keep it empty so that her cousin could use it as a dance studio; but this hadn't worked out. She gave Rose specific instructions as to when to come for her caretaking duties: the day after tomorrow, in forty-eight hours. She said she would leave a letter behind to instruct her what to do.

As soon as Rose had left with her little cart, Angel sat down to write that letter of instruction. She told Rose to contact Peter and gave her all the numbers where to reach him. Peter was the person who could be trusted to clear everything up with the minimum of fuss. Angel felt grateful to think how practical he was, and also to have inherited some of that quality from him. That was how it was easy for her now to take care of all the practical things to be done. She even remembered to write on Rose's note the approximate value of the pearl brooch and gold chain, so that no one would be able to cheat her over the price. Then she began to make her other preparations, and when they were complete, she sat down to write some more letters. However, these were more difficult, and finding that no words came to her, she gave up and wrote nothing. Her principal feeling was that a great promise had been made and broken, although it was not clear whether she herself had made and broken it, or whether this had been done to her. But the least she could do now was keep her promise to Lara.